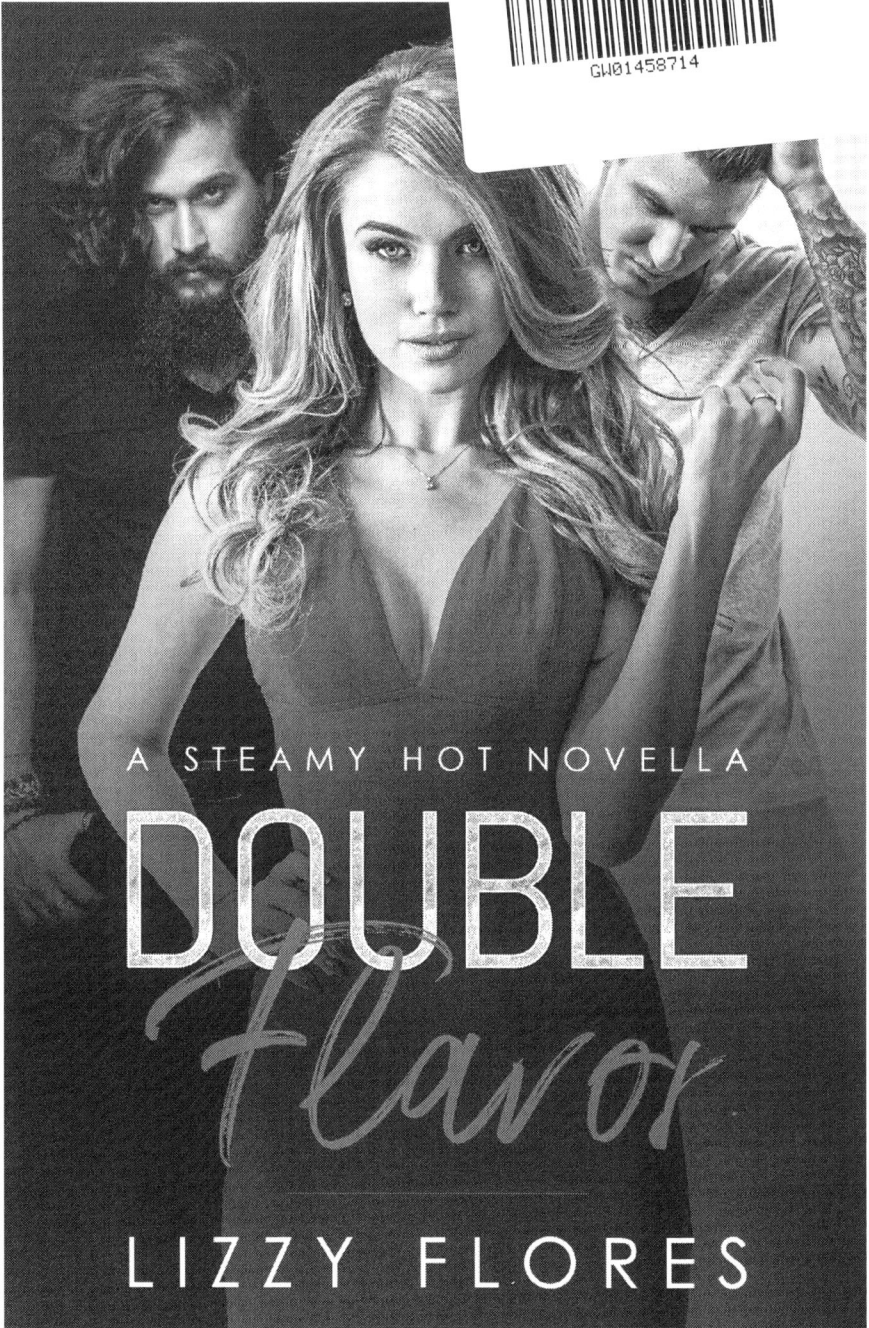

A STEAMY HOT NOVELLA

DOUBLE
Flavor

LIZZY FLORES

DOUBLE

FLAVOR

Copyright

The information presented in this report solely and fully represents the views of the author as of the date of publication. Any omission, or potential misrepresentation of, any peoples or companies is entirely unintentional. As a result of changing information, conditions or contexts, this author reserves the right to alter content at their sole discretion impunity.

The report is for informational purposes only and while every attempt has been made to verify the information contained herein, the author assumes no responsibility for errors, inaccuracies, and omissions. Each person has unique needs and this book cannot take these individual differences into account. For ease of use, all links in this report are redisrected through this link to facilitate any future changes and minimize dead links.

Contents

CHAPTER 1

Hi, my name is Skyler Jamison. I am a 28-year-old career woman, have short honey blonde hair with hazel eyes. My friends think I am fun but need to get out more, but I hate the whole situation of meeting strangers. Yes, my friends were also strangers before but they are friends now. I did not go out to meet them, they came in to meet me. I hate situations that I cannot control.

Did I tell you that I am single? Well-was single, and now I am in a situation that I cannot control, it has left me undecided but the funny part is I LOVE IT!

I sat there, swinging my legs as I drained my beer. The music was great but I just was not in the mood to dance. I am never in the mood to dance, I frowned. Well, only if they played my favourite songs, and they were about a handful. Why did I agree to this shit! Turning, I spotted one of my friends right in the middle of the dance floor, grinding on a man she had just met. I shook my head, they looked as though they were getting it on right there on the dance floor. And who could blame Sasha? The dude was fine, if you like that surfer dude look.

I took another swing at my beer, only to find it empty. 'Another please,' I called at the bartender. I turned and scanned for my other friend, Taylor. She was probably somewhere in a dark corner getting cozy with one of the guys as well. Sometimes I wished I was more like them, free and not too uptight.

'Here you go,' the bartender called.

Turning I frowned as he placed a red drink in front of me. 'What's this?'

'It's a sweet-tart lollipop martini. A gentleman over there sent it over,' I followed where his finger was pointing. Sitting there, with a tooth smile was a man, maybe in his early 30's with shaggy sandy hair, an undone black tie and a gray suit jacket. He lifted his glass to me but I ignored him. Turning to the bartender I raised my eyebrows at him. 'Well, it contains Barcadi lemon rum and...'

'Stop!' I raised my hand to him. 'May I please have a beer. A beer! Not some funny colored drink, just a beer. Simple and easy.' I took the drink and pushed it to a woman who had just come to the bar. 'Here, this is for you from that gentleman over there.' I took my beer and got off the stool.

Walking through bodies that were grinding on the dance floor was not easy but with determination I made it to the other side of the bar, away from Toothy-smile. Finding an empty chair, I pulled it and sat. Not five minutes passed before my friend Taylor came falling on me from behind.

'Sky, there you are!' she giggled as she slumped down on the seat next to me. 'It's hot in here!' she said as she fanned herself. Taking my beer, she downed what was left of it. 'You are supposed to be having fun, doll, it's your birthday today!'

I smiled and shook my head. Taylor Benjamin has been my friend for over eight years now. We met in college, one day at the cafeteria, oh so long ago. Details of our meeting? Well, it all started with a packet of gum and a can of soda. I see you seem confused. I had a packet of gum but wanted soda, she had soda but wanted a packet of gum. And the rest is as they so rightly put it-history.

'I know and I am enjoying myself,' I grabbed my bottle back and swung it in front of her face. 'Where is your dance partner anyway?'

'Took a bathroom break,' she leaned in and semi whispered. 'Did you check him out? Damn, he is fine! Hot steel buns under those trousers of his, I just couldn't take my hands off them!'

'I saw,' I laughed as Taylor laid her head on the table and groaned. 'Hey, don't go sleeping on the table, you heard!'

'Sleep?' Taylor's head shot up. 'Who said anything about sleep? I am waiting for my dark chocolate to get here so we go finish what we started at his place!'

I laughed, 'you sex-craved bitch!'

'You don't mind, do you?' she reached out and held my hand. 'This being your birthday and all.'

'Of course not,' I reassured her. 'You go get your groove on and we will meet tomorrow afternoon.'

'Why not morning?' she frowned.

I raised my eyebrows at her, 'will you really be up in the morning, Tay?'

She giggled and shook her head. 'Oh my gowd! Here he comes! Yummy!' she licked her lips dramatically.

I shook my head and turned to see her chocolate man.

'Don't look!' Taylor hissed. 'He will know we are talking about him.'

I ignored her, 'he already knows that, Tay, we are girls. It's in our nature to check out our friends' sex partners of the night,' I mumbled as I checked him out. He was tall, easily 6'4 with muscles in all the right places, his clothes made sure you saw them. His hair was cut military style, no piercing, no visible tattoo.
'Are you done checking me out?' he drawled as he stood right in front of me.

I shook my head, 'nope. I was told you had some hot buns. Mind turning around so I can check them out?' I heard Taylor groan. 'What? It's my birthday so I can do anything I want.' I giggled as both Taylor and her chocolate man made sounds. 'Meaning I can look at his buns, you dirty minded twerps!'

'In that case,' he said as he turned.

I touched one and nodded, 'steel. I'm Skyler, by the way.'

He turned and offered me his hand, his brown eyes dancing with amusement, 'Travis. And happy birthday, by the way.'

'Thanks,' I said, standing up. 'I got to head home now and get rid of these beers in my head. I have a document I need to send out before 10.' I scanned the room for Sasha. 'Please say bye to Sasha for me. Remember, tomorrow at 1. That should give you enough time,' I reached out and hugged Taylor. 'Be careful,' I whispered to her. 'See you around, Travis.'

Walking out of the club I took a huge breath of the fresh air. It was a cool autumn night but the stars were bright. Pulling my denim jacket closer I made my way to my car. Getting there I fumbled with my bag. 'Fucking key!' I mumbled as I got it and pulled it out. As if the key had a mind of its own it slipped from my hands and fell to the ground. I closed my eyes and groaned, 'seriously!' I bent and picked it up.

'Need any help?' a voice from my right drawled. I turned but couldn't really make out his face because of lack of lighting. He was tall, though, just like Travis but I could not be sure. Dropping his cigarette and stepping on it he walked slowly towards me. His steps were sure and ⬚uiet, like a jungle cat stalking its prey. I looked up at him when he stood in front of me. 'May i?' he raised one dark eyebrow at me.

Looking down I noticed his outstretched hand. My hand moved on its own volition and placed my car keys in his. I took in a deep breath, taking in as much of his scent in my lungs as I could. He smelt good. All clean male, with a hint of tobacco from the cigarette he had been smoking. I watched as he leaned in slowly, his blue-green eyes catching the lights from a passing car. The fleeting lights gave me few minutes to study his face. His hair was cut short, blond but darker than mine. Opening my door, he turned his face towards mine, a smile playing on his gorgeous lips and I could feel my nipples hardening.

You need a good fuck session; I reprimanded myself as I watched him straighten up.

'It's open,' his voice was deep, sexy and what a woman would like to listen to in the comfort of her bed.

Clearing my throat, as it had gone dry all of a sudden, I smiled as I took my key from him, 'Thanks.'

With a nod and a wink, he started to walk away from me. 'Wait!' I called before I could stop myself. He stopped and turned, his eyebrow going up again. Oh that was just soo sexy! 'Uhm, you come here often?' I rolled my eyes at myself. How cheesy could I get?

His lips broke into a small smile, just a hint of it, 'maybe,' was all he said as he walked back into the club.

I stood there for few seconds, watching his retreating back, wanting to run after him and taste those lips, run my hands over his solid body. Shaking my head, I groaned as I got into my car and drove away.

I do not have to tell you I had a sleepless night, which is pretty obvious. My mind kept going back to that hunk I met outside the club the previous night. As the morning light broke through my curtains I was thankful, the torture was just too much! Quickly, I grabbed a shower and dressed into my favorite home get up denim hot pants and a white t-shirt that tended to fall off on one shoulder. Grabbing a bowl of cereal, I walked to my study and started my computer. For the next two hours passed with me glued to my desktop.

'I am done for the day, Sky,' a lady in her mid-forties, with greying black hair stood by the door.

I smiled and waved, 'Thanks, Maria. Say hi to James for me, he doesn't want to visit me anymore.' Maria was the lady who cleaned my house for me. Yes, my job paid that good and it was something I enjoyed doing. I was not the boss yet but I was about two doors down from that room.

'He is busy with school now.' She defended her son. He was such an adorable little man, head full of black curls, sparking dark eyes, and a dimple that I lived to kiss. 'Will do,' Maria smiled and walked away.

Stretching, I pressed "send" and watched as the document was being uploaded. After Maria left I had taken a short break before continuing with my work. I had been busy with work for another two hours before I was finally done. After it was sent I stood up, checked the time and ran to my room to change, I had thirty minutes to meet up with my girls.

'You are late!' That was the greeting I got from Sasha as I joined her on our table. She had huge sunglasses on, making her pixie face seem smaller. She had her curls in a loose ponytail.

I placed my handbag on the side of my chair and smiled, 'I am sorry. When did you get here?'

She glanced at her watch, 'a few minutes ago.' A groan escaped her as a driver passed with his horn blazing. 'Tell that bastard to keep it quiet! Why did you let me drink that much?' she as accused me.

I rolled my eyes on her, 'me! I couldn't get you to listen to me for two minutes last night! Where is Taylor? She had said she will be here by 1pm.'

Sasha sat up and glanced over my shoulder. A smile broke on her face, 'having a last taste of her chocolate man. Those two had better find a room.'

Turning I looked at where Sasha was pointing. She was right. The two were going at it as though they had not seen each other the past twelve hours. They were standing behind a black jeep. What caught my eye and held it was not the car or my friend having her lips eaten out for the whole world to see. It was the guy who was standing outside the jeep, on the driver's side with a cigarette between his fingers. He had his face tilted to the other direction but I knew who he was.

Memories of the night before came back like a flood. The images that made me toss and turn the whole night played in my head until I had to press my thighs together tightly. A sigh escaped as the fabric of my panties moved on me.

'Yo, Tay, get a room!' Sasha called, immediately regretting it with a frown and a groan as she held her head in her palms. I turned back to her, 'are you alright?'

'No!' she groaned. 'This is a motherfucker of all hangovers! Well, at least I got her attention. Here she comes.'

I turned back, watching as Taylor made her way towards us, but the jeep was nowhere to be seen. I stifled a disappointed groan and forced a smile as Taylor came bouncing, a big grin on her baby face. 'You look well loved,' I commented as she sat and took a sip from Sasha's water.

'Oh, I was!' she leaned and gave me a kiss, before kissing Sasha's lowered head. 'Travis is AMAZING! Kept me up most of the night-well, what was remaining of it anyway! And believe me sex is the best medicine for a hangover,' she glanced at Sasha when she groaned even louder. 'What's up with you?'

'She didn't have enough sex to cure her hangover,' I supplied.

'Ha ha ha,' Sasha sat up and gulped on her water. 'Brandon-Landon or something had to leave early.' As she finished her sentence her mobile phone started to ring. Checking the number her smile grew, 'it's Landon,' she said with a smug smile before receiving the call.

'Soooo, what did you get up to last night after you left?' Taylor leaned in and smiled at me, cutting off Sasha as we knew she was going to talk forever.

I shrugged as I scanned the menu that was placed before me, 'got home, had a nice hot soak in the bath, scented candles and all the trimming before curling up on my bed and sleep.'

Taylor picked on a grape from the fruits displayed on the table and popped it in her mouth. This is why we loved coming to this place. It was not a big restaurant, sort like those that you find in France or Italy, where one could choose to sit inside or outside. We loved the outside, watching people go on with their lives. Oh, and the tables were always packed with munchies, from fruits to nuts to hot and fresh buns, whatever you fancied. And their food was just heaven! They had dishes from all over the world being served, which was amazing provided that it was not such a huge place.

'Really now?' she wiggled her eyebrows at me.

'You know something I don't?' I frowned at her.

She smiled, 'maybe.' She pushed her urban hair away from her face. 'Do you know a Jayden?'

I shrugged as I shook my head. Looking up I smiled at the waiter, 'I will have your world famous Lad na, and for this one here,' I pointed as Sasha who was busy giggling on the phone, 'bring in some chicken noodle soup. Taylor?'

'I'll have the Lad na as well,' she said with a smile before turning to me. 'Well? He seems to know you because he told me to say hi to you before they left.'

A light bulb went on, 'oh, you mean Travis' friend? He helped me with my car keys yesterday, they had a mind of their own.'

'Is that so?' Taylor's brown eyes lit with interest.

'No,' I said sharply. 'I know that look, Tay, don't even think about doing something funny.'

'What? You need a good screwing and who better than that hunk of a man? If my taste was into someone like him, I would have had him last night. But.'

'You like your man tall, muscled and chocolate,' I rolled my eyes as we both broke out to giggles.

'What?' Taylor shrugged unapologetic. 'I am a chocolate addict.'

Since I started knowing Taylor all those years back, she had never dated a Caucasian, which was different with me and Sasha. Between the two of us we have dated all the races found in the world, and we enjoyed each one of them.

'What did I miss?' Sasha placed her phone on the table and smiled at us, her brown eyes sparkling.

'If I didn't know better I would have said you just had phone sex with Landon,' Taylor sipped on Sasha's water again. 'Anyway, I was telling Sky that she needs a good turn on the sack. It's been how long now since her last boyfriend?'

Sasha held up one finger, 'and counting.'

'How she does it, it's beyond me,' Taylor made a face as she tried to figure it out. 'No one night stands, no friends with benefits, you will have cobwebs down there!'

And that was Taylor. She was the most talkative of the three of us, her reasoning was sometimes a bit on the crazy side but she was always ready to give advice, in her own Taylor kind of way. Sasha was not a talker, but when she decided to talk, people listen. She was charismatic, her words though not often heard, were craved.

'I doubt it!' I answered loudly, making a few people turn our way. Bending my head, I hid my face.

Taylor smirked, 'anyway, she met someone yesterday. He is Travis' friend.'

'Really,' Sasha giggled. 'Finally!'

'We did not meet, he just helped me with my keys and it was dark so he might not have seen me that well because I definitely didn't see him that well,' I bit on my lower lip for that little lie.

Sasha and Taylor looked at each other before breaking into laughs. I rolled my eyes and smiled. I knew my friends, and this was not a good sign. They were going to do something that will either upset me or make me laugh. 'Enough of that for now. Let me enjoy my lunch peacefully without the threat of indigestion.'

That evening as I was getting ready to go out with Taylor and Sasha, my mind kept turning to a blue-green eyed man. Standing back I checked myself in the mirror. I had decided on a full black outfit. Black skinny jeans with a black tank top, adding some color with my blood red heels, a touch of pink lip-gloss, not a fan of lipstick with eyeliner and dark eye shadow finished my look. My hair was easy, I had washed it and blow dried it to a soft finish. Giving myself a thumbs up I collected my red clutch bag and was about to get my car keys when my phone rang.

'Sky, we are outside,' was Taylor's greeting when I picked up.

'Ok, let me just collect my car keys,' I replied as I looked around my room.

There was a giggle and a laugh in the background before Taylor was back on the phone, 'no, dummy. Leave your car, that's why we are here to pick you up. Wanna see you with your hair down today?'

'Are you sure?' I asked, holding my keys and playing with them. I really did want to have fun tonight, and not worry about the driving.

'Yes!' a collective reply came. I could make Taylor's and Sasha's voices and what seemed to be Travis and Landon.

'Ok, already! I don't want to go deaf with that chorus. Let me just lock up and I will be down in a sec,' I disconnected the call and placed my car keys in the safe behind my bathroom mirror. A friend of mine was the one who chose that place, saying that no one ever thinks of looking there. Mind you, my neighborhood is safe. I have been living in the same place for the past four years and never heard about a break in. But, as my foster mother used to say, you could never be too careful. And yes, I was a foster child. My parents died when I was pretty young. Dad died first of a heart attack and mom followed a year after. I guess she could not cope with the death of her husband. I was one of the lucky few who is placed in a great home where you are given every opportunity to better yourself. I thank God every day for what Mrs. Shaw did for me, and pray that she is in heaven where she belongs.

After collecting my red crop jacket and activating the alarm, I walked out and locked my door. On the opposite of my drive parked the same jeep I had seen Taylor coming out from just a few minutes ago. Steering myself from rolling my eyes I commanded my legs to move, knowing full well this was a carefully-if not subtle-laid plan between Taylor and Sasha to get me with Jayden. And speaking of Jayden, he had his eyes on me the whole time I made my way to the car, making my knees feel like knocking together.

'You sit in front with Jayden,' Sasha told me as I got to the door, she was cuddling with Landon. 'We are making out at the back so you keep Jayden company in the front seat.'
Rolling my eyes, I opened the door and jumped in. 'Hi,' I smiled at Jayden as I told my heart to cool it down. In the space of two seconds I took in his appearance, and I nearly drooled. He was dressed in black denim with a grey shirt that was a bit tight, showing his ripped muscles. I couldn't see his shoes. Catching myself, I looked up only to blush and turn away when I met up with his eyes.

Jayden tilted his head and raised an eyebrow, 'good?'

I smiled as I looked out of the window and nodded, 'good.' My voice came out breathless and I closed my eyes.

The place we chose to go, well coerced by the guys, was a new and upcoming club. A lot of the young people found it a great place. It had VIP areas as well as a restaurant right at the top floor. It was just great. After discarding our jackets, the ladies and I headed to the restroom to freshen up.

'You bitches are going to pay for this,' I growled at them playfully.

They broke into laughs, hugging me from each side. 'You will thank us tomorrow when you wake up all sore and happy after a night full of passion in those huge arms of his.' Taylor placed a kiss on my hair and moved to the mirrors for reapplying her makeup.

'You will even skip your morning jog after the workout you are about to have tonight,' Sasha tickled me and moved away laughing. 'Serious, doll, you will be working on muscles that have been inactive for how long?'

'A year,' Taylor supplied as she turned and leaned on the sink, her pose accentuating a slim figure.

I rolled my eyes, 'ok fine! I am not going to say anything will happen tonight, so whatever will happen,' I shrugged as a small giggle escaped, 'but shit, that man is fine! I need to go dance off some of this sexual tension!'

When we got back to the club floor, we headed to the table the guys chose. We were VIP of course, a bit from the dance floor but we could see everything going on. Placing, our bags with the guys, we headed to the dance floor. Of all the three of us, Taylor was the best dancer. She just had the natural rhythm thing going on. I am not saying we were bad; we were just not as good as Taylor. She moved to all the different kinds of songs fabulously!

We had been on the dance floor for about fifteen minutes before taking a break and getting our drinks by our table. Taylor and Sasha decided to make out with their guys as I watched the people on the dance floor. Jayden was nowhere to be seen. After downing my beer, I went back on the dance floor, leaving the couple busy making out. When my favorite song hit the speakers I jumped up and laughed, Jack Back and David Guetta's Wild one two. Closing my eyes, I let the sounds carry me. It felt so freeing just moving, locking away everyone and letting the rhythm take you wherever it wanted you to go. I was so caught up with the song that when I felt someone's hands on my hips I gasped and tried to move away only to be pulled back.

'Relax, it's just me,' Jayden's voice whispered into my ears, causing the fine hairs all over my body to stand up with attention. I could feel my nipples hardening, becoming sensitive to the lacy bra I was wearing. I closed my eyes and leaned back on him, sculpturing my body to his. God, he was solid! With a sigh I let him lead me in the dance, only now realizing it had turned to some soft and slow song. He moved so gently, swaying me to the rhythm of the beats. His hands that were on my hips slowly moved and wrapped themselves around my waist. There was no inch left between us, we were that close.

I was thankful for the dark lights because I knew my face was flushed. Maybe my friends were right, maybe I just needed a good tumble on the bed with this hot bod and I might just flush him out of my system. Taking courage, I turned to face him, his arms never breaking apart, and placed my arms around him. I rested my head on his chest, listening to the beat and smiled. It seemed I was not the only one who was affected by our nearness. Moving back, I looked up at him, into his eyes. He was looking at me through hooded eyes, but I could see lust in those blue-green eyes of his and I knew that tonight, I was going to get some.

When the music stopped he took my hand and led me off the dance floor.

'We are heading out,' Jayden announced to the group. I looked at him and knew that I had no power to say no; actually, I did not want to say no. 'I'll talk to the guys to have taxis waiting for you by the counter.' And that was another thing that made this a club of choice. You could have transport provided for you if you wanted.

Taylor and Sasha both turned to me for confirmation and when they noticed my blush, they chuckled to themselves.

'See you tomorrow, Sky,' Sasha pulled me down to her. 'You go do all those naughty things you dreamt of doing to him last night,' she whispered with a knowing smile. I rolled my eyes on her and placed a kiss on her lips. I did not even ask her how she knew about my dreams, we just knew each other that much.

I walked to collect my jacket as Jayden went to arrange transport for the other couple inside. It was my first time to leave a club after only thirty minutes. I stood just outside the doors and looked up. The stars seemed to be smiling with me. I felt giddy, like a teenager on her first date with her crush.

An arm snaked around my waist and pulled at me. Warm lips placed a kiss on my neck and I had to fight hard to stop a shiver from running down my spine. 'Ready?' he whispered.

I was lost for word so I nodded. I let him take my hand and lead me to the car. When we got there, he walked me to the passenger side. Before I could get in, he moved me to the back door that was still closed and caged me with his arms.
He was so close as he tried to read my eyes, 'are you sure you want to do this?' His voice was low and husky.

I snuck my arms around his neck and pulled him the few inches that were remaining between us. My lips claimed his in a sweet torture that had his arms coming around me and pulling me against him. Even though I started the kiss, he 🄀uickly took charge. Running his fingers through my hair he held me in place as his lips devoured me. Oh, he was a good kisser. I could feel my legs quivering, my nipples rubbing on my bra, and between my legs... I just wanted him right there!
He moved from my lips to the side of my jaw before heading for my neck. A groaned escaped as his lips worked magic on me. His hands let go of my hair and moved to my hips, pulling me so I could feel the evidence of his arousal. I love this!

When I gasped as his lips moved further down, he reluctantly moved away from me and smirked. 'Ok, I got the answer. Let's get out of here!' he helped me get in, as my legs had suddenly turned to jelly-o before walking to his side and getting in.

As he opened the door to the main house from the garage I looked around. It was a typical man house, all in dark wood, chrome and white walls. It was simple but elegant, with all the trimmings of a man cave. His house was huge, open spaced area with monochromatic decorations. He flipped on a switch and the lights deemed.

'Would you like something to drink?' he asked as he dropped his keys and jacket on one of the sofas. He turned to me, his intense gaze making my breathe catch in my throat.

I shook my head, and placed my clutch bag on the nearest surface and turned to him. A drink was the furthest thing from my mind. I just wanted him, right there and then. 'Nice place you have here,' I said, barely recognizing my husky voice.

Jayden gave a small shrug and looked around, 'it's home. It was a studio, bought it for peanuts and did this.'

'Yourself?' I raised an eyebrow as my eyes wondered around the room.

'Yes,' he said as he started to walk towards me, his steps sure and confident. 'I like to get my hands dirty once in a while if it's something I will enjoy doing.' He stopped a foot away from me, his eyes hooded.

I swallowed, finding my mouth dry all of a sudden. Maybe I have been without sex for too long, I thought. I felt like a teenage girl on her first date. Biting my lower lip, I held his gaze, 'and what are some of the other things you like to get your hands dirty for?'

He gave me a lopsided smile, before hooking his thumbs onto my jeans and pulling me forward. I had to place my hands on his muscled chest to stop myself from tumbling over. 'How about I just show you?' he whispered into my ear, his breath hot on my skin, making all my fine hairs stand up to attention.

As he moved forward, I looked into his eyes, finding them fixed on my lips. Unconsciously, I ran the tip of my tongue on them, emanating a low groan from him. He raised a thumb and ran it over my slightly wet lip, before sucking it. 'You taste good,' he drawled softly, his lips forming that little smile that I had come to like. 'Do you mind if I have another taste?'

I shook my head, my hands taking a hold of his shirt. I was lost for words. All I wanted to do was to reach out to him and pull him to me, but I felt so weak, my legs barely supporting me. And all this was because of the hand that was playing havoc on my back. He was drawing circles on my back with one hand as the other was busy running over my face, neck, as though he wanted to keep the memory of my face in his mind.

When I saw he was not moving towards me, I groaned, 'please kiss me already!'

As though that was what he was waiting for, his lips descended on mine, taking them in a kiss so brutal yet so tender that blew my mind away. He was tentative at first, his mouth warm and lips softer than I remembered from the parking lot. My hands moved slowly up to his neck, taking a hold of his shirt collar and pulling him closer, if that was possible.

His tongue flicked out, tentatively running it on my lips before he deepened the kiss, extracting a low moan from me. Damn he was a good kisser! When his tongue flicked out the next time, I was ready, catching it between my lips and sucking on it slowly. It was his turn to moan as he pushed me backwards until I came in contact with the wall. With a low groan, he left my lips and moved to my jaw, giving my little nips with his teeth as he travelled to my neck. I closed my eyes and arched my back, throwing my neck backwards to give him more access. His warm lips travelled to the top of my breasts, as his hand moved from my waist to just below my right breast.

I could feel my nipples getting chaffed by the bra that I was wearing, and I just wanted it out. Jayden stopped kissing me, and rested his forehead on mine, his breathing heavy like mine.

'Why did you stop?' I whispered, because that was as loud as I could get.

He gave me kiss on my nose before taking hold of both my hands and pulling me with him, 'because if I didn't I was going to take you right here on the wall.'

I shook my head as I followed him, 'I don't mind,' I bit on my lower lip again. My goodness I just sounded like a hooker right there. I chanced a look on his face and found his eyes on me; his gaze was so hot that it made me squirm.

'For this first time,' he spoke softly, 'I want you on my bed. I want to make love to you tonight, the fucking will come later on.'

Oh, me! I smiled. There were going to be more times with him. I felt giddy, just like a teenager! We made our way to his bedroom which was up the stairs, stopping now and then to steal a few kisses. When we finally got up to his bedroom we both could not wait any longer. He pushed me to the nearest wall, his lips taking mine in a hungry kiss that took my breath away. My hands went up to his shirt and started to undo the buttons. When the last button was undone I removed his shirt and dropped it on the floor. My hands ran over his rippled body, my nails slightly scratching him, eliciting a moan from him. He broke off the kiss, only to remove my top and dropped it where his shirt was.

'Damn, you are beautiful!' he groaned as he attacked my neck once again, placing little nips before licking the pain away. His hands went to work on my jeans, as mine worked on his. It was a battle of who got who's off first. I giggled when I finally got his buckle undone and his jeans open. He moved backward and frowned.

I smiled at his confused look, pulling his head down I whispered to him, 'zipper at the back,' before arching my back away from the wall to give him space. I was rewarded with a nip on my lower lip.

'Cheater,' he mumbled as he unzipped my jeans and let them fall. He stood back to look at me. I felt over exposed, with my jeans pooled on my heels and I was left standing in my panties and bra. On their own volition, my hands started to move to hide my nakedness. He stopped them with his and shook his head, 'none of that. You're beautiful.'

I looked up at him, the desire in his eyes warming up my blood so fast I thought I was going to go up in flames. I took in his muscled body, the fine hair that disappeared into his briefs. 'So are you,' I smiled at him.

His hand let go of my hand and moved to my bra, a finger outlining the cups, before his thumb flicked on my nipple.

A gasp escaped me before I could stop myself. My legs felt like water, and I had to move back on the wall for support.

'Front?' he asked as he looked for a clasp of my bra.

I did not trust my voice so I nodded, and watched as his eyes darkened even more as they fell on my aroused nipples. They felt heavy under his gaze. His hand slowly cupped one, his thumb softly running over my nipple. I watched as his head lowered, his eyes still locked with mine to my other nipple. When his lips closed on it and suckled, I was thankful to the wall, as my legs nearly gave out on me. My arm went around his neck, holding him close as he took my nipple deep into his mouth, while his hand mimicked the movement on the other one.

'Jayden,' I moaned as his other arm snuck on my waist and pulled me fully to him. I could feel his erection through his jeans. Using my other hand, I removed his jeans completely, reached out and touched him. He was hot velvet over steel. I marveled at his size as my hand moved up and down his length, squeezing him to copy his mouth as it suckled on me.

He let go of my nipple and claimed my lips on a full on slaughter kiss that left both of us breathless. 'Shit, Skyler,' he groaned on my lips. 'I won't last if you do that.' He claimed my lips again as he carried me in arms and dropped me on his bed. He made a quick work of removing my shoes and the remainder of my clothes without once breaking the kiss. When I was finally void of all clothes he made a ⍰uick work on his before settling himself between my legs.

My hands were on his back, urging him on me. I loved his weight on me, his erection between my legs, rubbing on my thigh making me even wetter than I could remember being. I was close and I knew it. If he was not careful I was going to come just from his kisses alone!

'Please?' I do not even know what I was begging for, but I guess he understood. He reached for a foiled packet by his bedside and sat back on his legs. I watched him as he sheathed himself, licking my lips again.

Jayden moved forward and caught my tongue before it disappeared, sucking it into his. 'This tongue of yours is too tempting.' One of his hands moved to my thing, made its way slowly until it came to contact with what it was looking for. His fingers dwelled into my folds, making my hips shoot up and a moan escape from my parted lips. 'You are so ready for me!'

Before I could reply he entered me with one sure stroke, catching my gasp in a kiss. Oh, he felt good! I closed my eyes and savoured the moment, his slow withdrawal before sinking back into me with a force that had my breath catching in my throat.

'Open your eyes,' he commanded, gently. 'I wanna see your eyes.'

I opened my eyes and tried to focus on him. I gasped again as he withdrew to the tip before slamming into me again. I loved it! He took my arms and held them up above my head, giving him free reign of my breasts. He took my nipple into his mouth again, his suckling mimicking his thrusts into me.

'Faster,' I whimpered.

I was only rewarded with a smile but he never increased his tempo. I bend my legs and took him deeper, using the heels of my foot to try and push him faster into me but he resisted. My breathing was now coming fast, my body tightening around him. I closed my eyes and arched into him, pushing my nipple deeper into his warm mouth.

I moaned as he went deeper, his attention moving to my other nipple. He stopped moving and my eyes flew open. What the hell?

'Keep them open,' he said as he suckled faster and harder. He increased the tempo, moving faster and harder into me. His fingers laced with mine, holding me down, and his mouth a warm haven for my nipple.

'Jayden,' I groaned as my muscles tightened even more around him. His gaze was locked on mine and I just couldn't look away.

'Come for me, Sky,' he mumbled on my lips.

It was as if my body was waiting for that command from him. I came so fast and so hard it was bordering pain. My body shook, hands behind my head and mouth gapped. He caught my scream with his lips, my orgasm triggering his.

I woke up slowly, my groggy brain trying to assimilate where I was. I took in the grey curtains that were pushed away from the windows, letting in the early morning light. The sun was not even entirely up yet, but the scenery was spectacular nonetheless. I stretched my body and smiled as I felt muscles that were once asleep coming back to life. My friends were right; I had been long without good shag. And shagging it was! After the first slow as hell round, Jayden had increased his speed to Mach 3. We had moved through all the available surfaces in the room! From the fully carpeted floor to the wall, to the sofa that faced the bed and the shower wall. As I moved to get off the bed a hand on my waist stopped me. Turning I found Jayden staring at me.

'Where are you going, beautiful?' his voice was hoarse from sleep and the sexiest sound I have ever heard.

'I am sorry I woke you up,' I replied as I pulled the cover up, covering my bare breasts from his gaze, shy all of a sudden. 'I was just heading to the loo.'

He rolled over to his back, placed his arms behind his head and looked at me, 'Well?' When he saw I was not moving he raised an eyebrow, 'What are you waiting for?'

I pulled at the sheet, but found it stuck under him, 'may I have this then?'

'No,' he replied smugly. 'It's rather cool right now.'

I narrowed my eyes on him. He was teasing me, playing at my sudden shyness. Biting my bottom lip I made up my mind to get him back for what he was doing. Two could play that game. I pushed off the sheet completely, all the time keeping my eyes on him. I could have easily moved out of the bed from my side but I swung my leg over him, straddling him for a few seconds before swinging the other and getting off the bed. I smiled as I heard his quick intake of breath. Spying his shirt on the floor, I bent, picked it up and put it on.

'You are playing with fire, Sky,' his voice was husky, and when I turned to look at him his eyes were dark with desire.

'You had said it was a bit cool in here, ' I smiled innocently at him, 'besides, a little fire never hurt anybody,' I escaped to the washroom before he could do anything. After a quick use of the loo I was back in his room. I stood by the doorway, looking at him and thinking about the night that had passed. This was not me. I never slept with a guy on the first date. Heck, we were not even on a date!

'Come here,' he held his hand out to me. His gaze raking over my body and I watched as appreciation flare in his eyes.

Taking a deep breath to calm my nerves I willed my legs to walk to him. Getting by the bed, I took it, letting him pull me above him. He had such beautiful eyes, I thought to myself as we locked gazes. 'You good?' he pulled on my knees so that I was straddling him again, his hands staying on my thighs.

I blushed for a little, I could not help it, 'yes,' I replied hiding my face on the crook of his neck. I could feel his laughter vibrating his chest.

'We are a bit shy this morning,' he observed as he moved his hands to my hips, a little movement from him had me moving up and looking down at him. 'You are cute when you blush like this.' He moved one hand up, his fingers lightly brushing on my pink cheeks. 'I wonder what else I can do to get you looking so cute.' His hand traveled to my neck and he pulled my head down and kissed me, hard. He used his hand to keep me still as he grinded on me, making me aware of the arousal state of his manhood. It was pretty erotic as the only thing separating us being the sheet.

I moaned, giving his tongue access to mine. He took it, his tongue coaxing mine in a dance as old as time. He demanded my participation, and I gave it to him without hesitation. This was the way he loved me, no fucked me last night. He was rough, but exciting. He was wild, but gentle. And most of all he was a great lover I have ever had.

'Tell me you want me,' he demanded against my lips, his gaze locked with mine. His hand on my thigh had moved the shirt completely away from my body, running up and down as well as s ueezing my ass.

I gasped as he moved his hips up, his manhood coming to contact with my sensitive areas through the soft sheet. 'You know I do,' I groaned against his lips, trying to kiss him but he wouldn't let me.

He bucked up and rotated his hips, making my whole body quiver with anticipation. 'I want you to say the words. I want to hear them from these delicious lips.' He nipped on my lower lip.

'Don't do this to me!' I took hold of his hands and pushed myself down on him, this time making him hiss with the contact. 'Don't you feel it?'

One second I was above him, the next I was under him. My arms were placed above my head, held by one of his. The shirt I was wearing was removed in one fluid movement, leaving him free to cup one of my naked breasts. 'Oh, I feel it alright,' he lowered his lips to my nipple, taking it deep into his warm and moist mouth. 'Still need the words.'

'No.'

I could feel his smile against my breast, and I knew this was going to be as good as it gets. 'So be it.' He proceeded in torturing me with his hands and lips, arousing me to the point of causing me to scream, but he never moved to enter me. Frustrated, I moved my hips up, cradling him between my legs. 'Jayden, please!'

'You know what you are supposed to do,' he mumbled on the crook of my neck. 'And I will give you what you want,' he flexed his hips, bringing him right against me. 'I'll give you exactly what you need. Just say the words, Sky.'

I moaned, tried to break off his hold on me but couldn't. I was breathless, aroused beyond reason and the only thing left for me to say was, 'I want you,' I said. 'I want you right now!'

CHAPTER 2

He groaned as he moved the sheet away. Without stopping, he turned me onto my stomach and using his hands he pulled my hips up. I was on my hands and knees, my torso resting on the bed with my ass up in the air and ready for him.

'Damn it, Sky,' he grunted. 'You are driving me crazy!' he pushed into me, getting a cry from me and a hiss from him. Oh, he was hungry! Deep thrusts that had me gasping for air. I could feel my body tightening around him, pulling him even deeper, as deep as I could.

'Don't stop,' I reached my hand behind me, holding his thigh and pulling him close. I could feel the tension build, that feeling of an uncontrolled shiver coursing through me. A sob escaped my throat. This was different from the first orgasm I had in his arms, totally different from the second or third. This one right here, was the result of the hard grinding that I was being given. And when it hit, it left me breathless, a silent sob in the pillow, my fingers bunching the bed sheet. When I felt him tense behind me I moaned his name out, 'Jayden!' My knees gave way and I collapsed on the bed, taking him with me.

He was not heavy, just heavenly. He moved a bit, his head moving on the pillow besides me. He reached up and pushed my hair back away from my forehead. He placed a kiss on it, his gaze locking with mine, 'spend the day with me.'

I smiled, that was the only thing that I could do, I had no energy. 'The girls... .'

'We will call them later,' his arms tightened around me. 'Say yes, Sky. Let's get to know each other.'

I could not help myself. I burst out laughing, 'I think we know each other very well, Jayden, don't you agree?'

He bit my lip and slapped my ass, 'away from the bed, lioness.'

I purred just for good measure. I looked up at him, holding his gaze seeing a fleet of emotions going through them. He had such beautiful, expressive eyes, and I couldn't wait to get to know him. 'I would like that very much,' I replied in a small shy voice.

It was way past eight in the evening when he finally dropped me at my house. He got out of his car and walked to my side, opening the car door for me. With his help I stepped out of the jeep and was about to start for the porch when he pulled me in his arms.

'I am not coming in,' he smiled at my disappointed look on my face. I really should learn how to mask my feelings. 'Not that I don't want to, it's just that I won't leave and you need your rest.'

I smiled, a slow smile, 'I understand. Thank you for today,' I said, my fingers playing with the buttons of his denim jacket. 'And yesterday. I had a great time.'

'Yeah, me too,' he leaned down and took my lips in his. I could have fallen to the ground if he wasn't holding me. Ok, so I am a drama ueen, but he was that good. He ended the kiss too quickly and my groan let him know. 'See you tomorrow night.'

I nodded and let him go, watched him enter his car.

'Go inside so I know you are safe, Sky,' he shook his head at me when he saw I had not moved an inch.

Feeling like a little girl, I pouted, turned around and walked slowly to my front door. Before entering I turned and blew him a kiss.

Just as I dropped my clutch bag on the side table my phone rang. 'Hello?'

'Good, you are back!' Taylor's voice sang from the other side. 'We will be right over!'

I shook my head as I replaced the receiver on the cradle. I had exactly fifteen minutes before they arrived so I ran to my room, had a little time to change and placed some popcorn in the microwave. Just as the time went off on the microwave, my doorbell rang.

'Details!' was Sasha's greeting as she made her way to the sitting room.

Taylor stopped in front of me and hugged me hard, 'you look radiant. Well loved,' she kissed me. 'It suits you.'

'Nice to see you bunnies too,' I rolled my eyes as we walked to the sitting room. Sasha was seated on the floor, her legs crossed below her.

'So, how is he?' she asked, her eyes dancing with excitement.

'How was Landon?' I counter asked her.

She shrugged, 'the boy is fine, doll! And he is packing,' she forged a shiver. 'His mouth works wonders. He does this thing with his tongue where he places it on my cl..'

'Whoa, enough details!' Taylor stopped her. 'Sky was just teasing you. No embarrassment bone in you!'

'It's a natural process, even animals do it!' Sasha defended herself with a shrug. 'Don't tell me you are not curious! She is a recycled virgin!'

'Recycled virgin?' I huffed as her. 'I will have you know that it has been in the game.'

'Using a dildo or whatever does not count, honey,' Sasha rolled her eyes. I turned to Taylor for help but she just shrugged and smiled.

'I agree,' she said. 'Besides, I already told you that Travis was the best, still is!' she turned to me, 'so spill!'

I looked at my friends and knew that they will not leave me alone until they knew everything. I took a deep breath, praying that I don't blush because then I won't hear the end of it. 'He is amazing, that's all I can say.'

'Oh, bitch please!' Taylor rolled her eyes on me 'A movie can be amazing, shoes are amazing, clowns are amazing but a man is not described by that verb.'

'We want the juicy stuff,' Sasha proclaimed around a mouthful of popcorn. 'You know, how is he hung? Is he great at using his e◌uipment? That is what we want to know.'

I laughed. 'You really are forward, hey! I am not going to tell you all that because I know every time you see him you will be envisioning him and his equipment. Just like the way I do when I see your boyfriends.' They both gasped, feigning shock. 'Don't even think of pretending you don't do this!'

They both broke into laughs, 'we are just teasing you, honey,' Taylor replied. She looked at me, her eyes becoming serious. 'We know you, Sky. You are not a one-night stand girl. So, is it serious?'

'I don't know,' I replied truthfully. And I really didn't know. Yes, I was not a one night stand girl, I just did not buy into the whole sleep with a stranger you pick up at the bar concept. But there was something about Jayden that called to me, something that I could not control. It seemed to be telling me to breakdown all those inhibitions I had about relationships and just go for it.

Sasha stood up and came to where I was seated. Taking the space besides me, she took my hand, 'what is it, Sky?'

I shrugged and shook my head, 'it's like there is something that is pulling me to him, guys. I can't stop myself. I don't know how he feels and at this moment in time, I really don't care. I just want him.' I looked at my friends, seeing the understanding in their eyes and that was enough for me.

Monday morning found me in the highest of moods. I did not know sex could act as a happy drug, and it seemed everyone in the office picked up on my good mood.

'You are happy today,' Harris stated as he took in my smile. Harris Fields was the go to guy when you had issues with your computer; he was available to us twenty-four /seven. Right now he was installing a new software on my desktop for me. We had been working together for the past seven months and if I said I did not notice the longing in his eyes, I would be lying.

But Harris was one of those guys that you put in a family zone, where you view them as a big brother or something, giving no opportunity for any hanky-panky business. 'I had a good weekend,' I replied as I perched on my desk. 'How long will it take?'

'Long enough for you to come and meet our new client,' my boss's voice said from the door. Mason Garson, love man in his fifties. He ran the best interior designing company in the country. He had set up the company with his life partner Simon, who decided to be a silent partner, when he was still very young and interior decorating was seen as a woman's career. But within a year of setting up, he had so many clients that he had to refuse others. And so it grew and grew and grew! 'Come on, darling.'

'But I am not done with the other three you gave me,' I complained. I had a right to, the projects he had given me were of huge magnitude, one was renovating a holiday lodge which had about five different cottages, another was revamping an old hose from the bottom and the other was of transforming what was once a hotel into a school. And once you are given projects like that, you are excused from doing any other projects.

'We will just send one to Sarah's way,' he waved my complaint away. 'This one is not a huge project but it's rather very important. This client wants only the best.'

I laughed and placed my hand through the crook of his arm. Ours was a informal working environment, where we teased and joked but always made sure that our work was top notch. 'Did you just admit to me that I am your best employee?'

'Don't let it get to your head,' he warned with a smile as he held the door to his office open for me.

'Wouldn't dream of it,' I replied with a smile. As I entered, a man in a grey suit came to his feet. He was facing the other direction so I had no idea how he looked like. But his back was-wow! The suit he was wearing was tailor-made, for sure, as it accentuated his physic. I had to snap myself from staring at the man's ass. Shaking myself mentally, I forced my legs to move forward.

'Mr. Cadman, please meet one of my best designer, Skyler,' Mason introduced me as he walked to his desk. He sat down and motioned for me to step even further into the room. As I approached his desk, Mr. Cadman turned and smiled. My heart literally skipped a bit. He had the most arresting eyes I've ever seen. Blue as the skies. His lips turned up in a smile that might as well have been a shout for Yeah-I-know-I-am-handsome-look-away.

I schooled my features and extended my hand, 'Mr. Cadman,' I said, thankful that I still had my voice.

'Alex, please,' he took my hand in his.

I smiled and removed my hand as soon as it was polite to do saw. Curling it into a fist I tried to ignore the electric charge that had travelled up when our hands met, the same charge I felt when Jayden and I first touched. Swallowing a groan, I pasted a polite smile and sat. 'Alex Cadman,' I thought out loud, 'where have I heard that name before?'

'The Cadman Cancer Research Centre, the Cadman Children's World Foundation,' Mason supplied. 'But the most important one is that he is the CEO and owner of the Cadman Shipping.'

My brain linked the dots. He was old money for sure. The Cadman Shipping Company was started by his great grandfather way back and has been growing at a constant pace. The last report I heard about them was that they had increased their shipping base to twenty other countries around the world. 'Yes, that's where I heard it.' I looked at Mason expectedly, wanting to get to why I was needed.

'Mr. Cadman,' Mason smiled from the look he got from the man himself. 'Sorry. Alex wants to refurbish one of his country houses for his mother. She has recently suffered from a hip replacement surgery and he wants her to stay away from stairs and all that. That is where you come in. Alex has re?uested for you to accompany him to the estate tomorrow and decide what you want to do to it.'

I was curious about the house. I guess this is what made me good at what I did, and I am being modest about it. I loved my job, it was hard work and sometimes frustrating but there is nothing more exciting, more fulfilling than seeing your designs come to life. There are no words to explain how one feels when a client bursts into tears for making their dreams a reality. I lived for those moments. 'I am given free reign?' I could not hide my excitement from that fact.

'Yes,' Alex said. He was seated back on the chair, one of his legs crossed across the other. His posture itself spoke of money and confidence. 'I will try and get Mother's input but I think she will agree with me when I say we just want something that will make mobility easy for her. I will set a meeting with her for you so that you can talk about color schemes and material and whatever other designing tools you will need.'

I nodded, my mind still on the free reign part, 'uhm-so when you said free reign,' I started, getting a chuckle from Mason. 'What?'

'And this is why I said she will be the best fit for your project, Alex,' he smiled at me and then at Alex. 'Her mind is already turning in that beautiful head of hers. And you said the magic words.'

'Magic words?' Alex asked Mason though his gaze was on me. His blue eyes twinkled with something I could not understand. It excited me, but at the same time frightened me.

'Yes,' Mason nodded. 'Free reign. Every person in our business world loves to be given free reign to do anything they want. It makes the work done easier, rather than being limited by the client.'

Alex smiled and turned to Mason, 'That is true.' He glanced at his watch and stood up, 'I have to go now. Are you free this evening? We could meet up and discuss a few aspects that you would want to bring forth.' he asked me.

Not prepared for the question I nodded, then groaned and shook my head, 'no, I am not today. Though we can have a meeting tomorrow if that's alright?'

There was something dark in his eyes for a few seconds after I answered but it disappeared quickly, making me think I had imagined it. 'I will call you tomorrow then,' he shook Mason's head before giving me a small acknowledging nod before he walked out.

'Well,' Mason said. 'What do you think?'

'About the man or the job?' I asked, my eyes twinkling with mischief.

Mason laughed and pointed a finger at me, 'Simon would not appreciate that joke.'

I laughed out loud, 'warning taken. About the job,' I got down to business. 'Let's see tomorrow and I will let you know. However, just the thought of having free reign on the house, I love it already!'

Mason laughed, 'I knew you would be interested. Now, make the necessary arrangements with Sarah to take over one of your projects, I don't know which one you want to let go and I really don't care as you have done. Tomorrow meet with Alex. I am sure he will take you to the house so you have the whole day off and come up with your plans. I want your first plans on my desk by Thursday. You know the rest.'

I knew I was being dismissed. Standing up I made my way out of his office to my own. As I sat down my mobile phone rang. Without checking the caller id, I answered, 'hello?'

'Hi, lioness,' Jayden's sexy voice came through the phone.

I smiled and sat back on my chair, 'Hi yourself.'

'I was just thinking of you,' he said. 'Can't wait to see you later on.'

For a few seconds I felt guilty, I had been eyeing another man when I had just started a relationship with another. I did not even know if I was in a relationship with him or not. That was something that we will have to talk about later on. 'Are you sure you want to make dinner? I could come early and help you cook.'

He laughed, low and husky. So sexy that it made me hot all of a sudden, 'are you scared I am going to poison you?'

'Well,' I started, teasing him. I laughed when I heard his growl. 'Down boy. Ok, ok, I will eat whatever you will prepare for us. Do I need to bring anything?'

'Just your sexy ass,' he said. 'I have plans for that after dinner.'

I laughed, 'desert, am I?'

'You said it,' he said. I could hear voices from the background. 'I have to go. See you soon.'

I hung up and leaned back on my chair, thinking of what will happen tonight or two days from today. Jayden was a great guy; I could see myself with him. He was my kind of guy, always reserved but lets it all out in bed. For some unknown reason, my mind turned to Alex and his gaze when he looked at me. I remembered feeling the heat pooling in my underwear. Closing my eyes, I tried to block the images of me and Alex in less than conventional poses.

'Sarah!' I called from my office, better to get the handover now so that I can go for lunch with the girls.

'Guys, I am in trouble!' was my greeting when I sat down at one of our favourite lunch spot. The great thing about working close to your friends is that you get to unwind and eat with others.

'Doll, you can't know now,' Sasha rolled her eyes. 'You have to wait until you miss your ps.'

I frowned at her, confused. 'What?' Then her meaning sunk in, making me shake my head, 'no, not that! I mean men trouble?'

'Already?!' Taylor looked shocked, 'You've just been with the guy one night, one night and already in trouble. What has he done?'

I groaned and hid my face in my hands, 'will you two listen to me first before you jump into your own conclusions?' When I had their full attention I smiled, 'thank you.' I kept ⬚uiet, trying to collect my thoughts.

'Speak already!' Sasha was never big on patience.

I took a deep breath and started, 'I don't know what I am going to do. I like Jayden, I really do. He is fun, sexy and a great lover.'

'So what's the problem?' Taylor frowned, her confusion written all over her face.

'Today I got called to Mason's office. We have a new client, mighty big client,' I bit my lip and lowered my eyes.

Sasha sighed and groaned, 'get to the point, doll!'

'I am sexually attracted to him,' I said in a rush. 'We shook hands and an electric current went up my arm. I have been thinking about him this whole morning. But I am also thinking about Jay-also sexually-and I just don't know what to do!'

For a few seconds my two best friends just stared at me with blank faces, before turning to each other and bursting out laughing.

My mouth hung open with disbelief, 'guys!! This is a crisis right here!!'

'Oh, doll!' Sasha wiped tears from the corner of her eyes-yes, she was laughing that hard! 'That is what you get for staying sex free for a year and a half! What did you expect? You are hungry, little Skyler wants to play-or is it be played with-and your body is telling you that one isn't enough!'

I gasped, 'what! No! I can't do that!'

'Sky, baby,' Taylor reached out and held my hand. 'Are you and Jayden exclusive?'

'No, but.' I started, only to have Taylor shake her head on me.

'Then what's stopping you from having this new guy in the sack? You are not exclusive, meaning you are still allowed to be with other people. One night of great sex does not equalize to a relationship, honey.'

'But.' I started again but was interrupted by Sasha.

'No buts, Sky. When you and Jayden decide to be exclusive and you get these feelings, then that will be a problem. But for now, you have nothing to feel guilty about. He is probably banging another woman as well.'

My mind was trying to process what they were saying but I just couldn't grasp the fact that I was not the only girl that Jayden was sleeping with. There was a pain in my heart that I did not want to understand. Was I getting attached to him too ⸮uickly? How was I to act or react if he tells me that he is seeing other women? These were the reasons why I never had one night stands, I get attached to people too ⸮uickly and make up a relationship that is not there.

Going against my better judgement I looked up at my friends, 'so, what do you think I should do?'

'Depends,' Taylor shrugged and let go of my hand. 'Does he feel the same chemistry as you?'

I shrugged. I really did not know. Maybe I was overreacting. But there was something in his blue eyes that told me he was interested, but again how could I be sure?

'Find out! When are you meeting him again?'

'Tomorrow,' I mumbled, already getting scared of what my two friends were going to say. But what scared me the most was that I was going to do exactly what they tell me to do.

'At the office or somewhere else?' Sasha asked. 'Because if it's at the office, come up with an excuse to get it outside the office. From there it's pretty simple. Check his body language, his eyes, his lips-the whole lot. Don't worry, you will definitely know if he is interested or not.'

I bit on my lower lip, horrified with myself for even considering doing what they were telling me. But what would it hurt to get to know Alex, at the same time I get to know Jayden? I shook my head and sighed, 'I can't believe it but I will do what you say and keep you updated.' I smiled. 'But I will think of that tomorrow as today Jayden will be on my mind!'

I sat on the barstool sipping on wine, watching as Jayden placed the mushrooms onto the frying pan. He seemed so comfortable in the kitchen, moving effortlessly around.

'Sure I can't help you with anything?' I asked as I took another sip from my glass. I am not really a wine person and to me all dry wines tasted the same, all whites tasted the same. But for the first time I knew I was drinking some good stuff.

Jayden turned and looked at me. A sexy smile broke on his lips as he made his way to where I was sitting. Standing behind me, he swung my stool around so that I would be facing him. Taking my wine glass from my seemingly limp fingers he took a sip and bent over to place his lips on mine.

A groan escaped from my throat. To me there was nothing sexier than sharing a drink in a kiss. I opened my lips to him, allowing the wine to flow gently from his mouth to mine. Like a starved child I swallowed, running my tongue on his lips just in case there was a stray drop somewhere.

After all the wine was gone, Jayden claimed my lips in a fierce kiss; his hands on my thighs widened them so that he was standing between them. His lips played with mine, teasing them with small sucking motion and nipping that made me hot! I ran my hands from his chest to his neck, pulling him deeper into my embrace. I made a move to make the kiss deeper but he pulled away, removing my hands from his neck and holding them in his.

Resting his forehead on mine, he smiled. His sexy as hell smile making me hotter-and wetter-than I could have liked to be at that moment. 'You are so tempting, lioness.' He placed a kiss on my nose. I crinkled my nose, making him laugh. 'But as tempting as you are, I am hungry and so are you.'

'I am hungry,' I broke free from his hands and placed my arms around his neck once again, 'just not for food.'

He groaned and swiped down to claim my lips once again in a kiss so hungry and so fierce that it left me breathless. He ended it with a series of nips. 'Don't tempt me, lioness.'

I pouted and purred at him, making him throw his head back and laugh.

He shook his head, his eyes dark so filled with desire. 'For what I have planned for tonight, you need to be fed first.' He moved away from me before I could reach for him.

I swung my stool back around, took a sip of my wine and smiled at him, 'Promises, promises.'

He smiled and winked at me.

I sat back and breathed in. 'That was the best steak with mushroom sauce I have ever tasted! Compliments to the chef.' I raised my glass to him.

Jayden smiled and rested his arm on his raised knee. We were seated on the floor, overlooking a large floor to ceiling window that had the best view of the moon. He had dimmed all the lights, soft music played in the background-just perfect. 'I am glad you enjoyed it.'

'Where did you learn to cook like that?'

He gave a small smile, 'my foster sister. She is chef. Back then she used to make cooking a punishment. Me, a boy of thirteen years sitting in the kitchen dicing carrots and onions,' he made a face.

I smiled as I tried to come up with that scenario. 'I can bet. With the way you cook, you must have been in a whole lot of trouble.' I looked at him, trying to gauge his reaction. I did not want to push him for information.

I was relieved when a smile broke out of his beautiful lips, 'you have no idea! But I think by the time I was fifteen or sixteen I had already developed a love for food. I used to get in trouble on purpose so I could help Wendy in the kitchen.'

'I bet she knew that,' I smiled, thanking Wendy for her help. I am no master in the kitchen, in actual fact if I could I would just seal that room up in my apartment. Don't get me wrong, I don't hate Cooking-I just find it cumbersome. Cutting this, dicing that! If I had a person to get all my ingredients ready, I would cook day and night!

'She must have,' Jayden nodded. 'Because from 'get your ass in the kitchen now!' it became 'kitchen, Jayden' said with a smile. And I did not have to dice the onions only this time. I could add a pinch of salt, stir something.'

'My bad security man is a chef,' I teased him. I leaned back and moved my leg to his side, nudging him with my toes. 'Who would have thought?'

'Only you know that secret,' he placed his drink down and reached for my leg. Slowly he ran his thumb across my foot, making my toes curl. He did it again, this time focusing on the ball of my foot. He made small circular motions with his fingers on the ball of my foot, all the while his eyes holding mine. He moved his hand up and down my foot, his fingers going in circles up and down.

I leaned my head back and sighed. His hands were like magic, they felt so good! After five minutes on one leg, he reached for the other, giving it the same attention as its twin. I could not help myself; I leaned all the way back, laid down and closed my eyes. As his hands worked on my feet I could feel my stomach muscles tightening, my nipples hardening. I smiled a little when I felt him place a kiss on the center of my foot, my toes curling up

'That's ticklish,' I mumbled, keeping my eyes closed. He did it again and took a nip on my big toe. I gasped and opened my eyes. He was looking at me, intensely, his eyes dark with sexual hunger. 'Ticklish,' I said again, my voice husky.

He gave me a lopsided smile. His hand started to travel from my foot, up my leg. His palm was so warm, massaging me as it travelled up. Still holding my gaze, his lips started to follow his hand, placing kisses from my ankle, up on my calf and stopped on my knee. He looked at me as he pushed my dress up, exposing my thighs to his hand and his mouth.

Running his hands softly upwards, he placed kisses on my thighs, wringing a low moan from me. 'Jayden, what are you doing?'

'I want my dessert,' he mumbled on my thighs. His hands were now on my hips. My dress was bunched on my waist, my black lacy v string panties there for him to see. He smiled at me. 'I like these,' he traced the panty outline with his fingers. With one move, he moved me up and away from the plates that were still on the floor between up. He stretched out before me, resting between my opened legs. 'I might just keep them with me,' he mumbled as he leaned forward and blew on me.

I gasped. I did not know I was already wet, or that I was that sensitive that a blow of air could cause sensations all the way up my body. 'Jayden!'

'All in good time,' he mumbled as he placed kisses on the insides of my thighs. He moved his lips and grazed on me gently through my panties, running the tip of his tongue on me.

I groaned and bucked against him, I could not help myself. I moved to place my hands on his head but he was ᑫuick. Taking a hold of my hands, he held them prison on my side. 'Jayden...'

'Yes?' he looked up at me as his tongue came out once again and licked me through my panties. 'What do you want, lioness?'

'I..' a low groan escaped as the tip of his tongue stayed on me, making small flicks that were driving me crazy. 'You know what I want,' I said breathlessly. I moved my hips, trying to draw him closer. 'Jayden!'

He let go of one of my hands and moved it to my panties, hooking it with his thumb. Keeping his eyes on me, he slowly and gently started to pull it off. I wiggled, trying to help him remove it faster. Within seconds I was bare for him to see. 'I am keeping this,' he said as he placed my panties in his denim pocket. Taking his position once again, he took hold of my hand and held it to my side. His eyes hooded and intense he leaned forward. He placed a kiss on my pelvic, moving slowly to my belly button before he moved downwards

Once his lips were on me all thought went out of the window. He started with just the tip of his tongue on me, flicking me up and down and then doing a circular motion with it. I gasped and tried to sit up, watch what he was doing, but he was holding my hands firmly. He looked up at me as he placed his full mouth on me. I could not help it, I bucked up and groaned.

'That's it,' he whispered, 'let go.'

I shook my head side to side and closed my eyes. He let go of my hands and took hold of my hips, pulling me closer to his administrations. The sensations travelled through my body, making it hard for me to breathe. He started sucking me, as his tongue continued licking. I could feel it building inside me, something so intense that it had me shaking.

Jayden groaned, the sound riveting through my body. He kept the sucking motion in a rhythm, drawing me closer and closer to the edge. My eyes flew open and clashed with his; I tried to catch my breath but for some reason my throat could not work. I gasped as my body went up in fire. Pure and blissful yet so intense it bordered near pain! A long scream escaped me as my body bucked against his lips, my eyes rolled back and I let go.

Jayden placed a soft kiss on my forehead, prompting me to open my eyes and look up at him. Little shivers still ran down my body. He smiled as he placed a kiss on my slightly slack lips. 'That was the best dessert I have ever had.'

I smiled at him and shook my head, 'what about mine?' my voice was husky from desire, hoarse from the screams.

He leaned forward and kissed me once again. He took his time, running his hand from where it was resting on my stomach to just below one of my breasts. He moved his thumb slightly across it, wringing a hiss from me. My nipples were sensitive, been chaffed by the lacy bra that I was wearing. With a small nip he let go of my lips and stood up. Without a word he bent down and pulled me into his arms. This close to him I could feel how aroused he was, it brought a smile to my face.

'Smiling at a man's discomfort, lioness?' he leaned in and sucked hard on my neck.

In my head I was already going through way to hide the hickey he just gave me. 'I am just thinking of the ways I can make him comfortable again,' I said, rubbing him through his denim.

He groaned and placed his forehead on mine, 'what have you done to my world, Sky? I find I can't think of anything but you. What have you done?' he claimed my lips in a demanding kiss, as though the answer was there.

I let him kiss me, as I continued to rub him gently. If he thought his world was upside down because of me, then he was about to find out that mine was far worse.

He pulled me deeper into his arms, his hands like steel around me. He broke free when we both ran out of air. He placed his arms around me and moved us to the nearest wall, claiming my lips once again. I had to place both my legs and arms around for support. So fast I could not keep up, he undid his zipper, sheathed himself and was inside me before I could blink.

A gasp escaped me before it turned to a low moan. Damn, he felt good! For a few seconds, we did not move. He had moved from my lips and buried his face on the crook of my neck, heavy breaths coming from him. My hands on his back bunched his shirt, holding so tightly to him. Finally, he moved, slow and sure plunging into me.

He started to build up a rhythm, which I matched. My eyes closed, there was only Jayden and I in the world at that time, no one else mattered, just us.

He moved his head from my neck and claimed my lips again, this time not as demanding but more teasing. His tongue darted out and teased mine. He ran in on my lips, placed kisses on the corner of my lips. His hands on my hips guiding me in the rhythm, slow movements that were picking up speed.

'You are mine,' he growled against my lips, his hands digging on my hips. He wasn't gentle, we were not making love. We were fucking and I loved it. 'Say it, Sky.'

'I am yours,' I gasped, as I felt the tension begin to grow once again in my tummy. 'Oh, God, Jayden! I am cumming again,' I whimpered as I pulled him closer to me.

'Let go for me,' he whispered as he increased his tempo yet again.

I had no control of my body. I felt it spiral out of control, with a gasp and another scream I let go, cumming so hard that I could see stars behind my tightly closed eyes. From far I heard a grunt and Jayden went still, just twitching a bit. I smiled and held him closer, breathing in our mixed scents.

'See what I mean?' he moved back so that he could look at my face. 'I lose control when I am with you, Sky. Something that I have never done before.'

I smiled at him and leaned forward, 'control is so overrated sometimes,' I mumbled against his lips before placing a kiss of my own there. Moving back, I tilted my head and really looked at him. His handsome face flushed from the pleasure we just shared. 'You do the same to me, Jayden,' I said with a smile, placing my hand on his cheek. He turned and placed a kiss on my palm. 'This girl is a very shy girl, but when she is with you she becomes someone completely different. You bring the best out of her.'

He smiled, 'I am glad.' I made a move to get off him but his arms stopped me. 'Don't.'

'We have to clean up the plates,' I gestured to the place where we had sat down to eat.

He swung me around and started for the stairs to his bedroom. 'I have someone who comes in the morning. She will clean up. Besides, I only have a few hours left with you before you head home. I wish this was a Friday.'

I smiled as I snuggled deeper into his arms. This was going to be a long night.

The next day I walked into the office with a big smile on my face, though I probably had about three hours of sleep the night before. Every time I was getting ready to leave, he would do something to stop me. And it was not only about the sex, we talked, got to know each other a little bit. We spoke about his time in foster homes, four of them in total. I told him about my life, being an only child to a mother who did not want to be a parent.

Yes, she had been there for me financially, put me through school, but the moment I was ready to stand on my own two feet, she had up and left. It has been six years and I have not heard anything from her, I am not even sure if she is alive!

'That smile!' Sarah commented as she fell into step with me. 'What were you up to last night?'

I laughed and winked at her, 'good girls never tell. So, how are you finding your new project?'

Sarah giggled, 'changing the subject, I see! Well, thanks to your excellent organizational skills everything is running smoothly. I just have to meet with the client today. How is she?'

I shrugged, 'she's alright. It helps that she knows exactly what she wants so it makes it easy to follow her instructions.' We stopped by her door. 'You do know that if you have anything you need help with, I am here, right?'

'Yes,' Sarah smiled. 'And that is why I am confident in this. If you decide to stay away from work, I might have panic attacks the whole day!'

I placed a comforting hand on her arm, 'if I did not think you could handle this, I wouldn't have given it to you. I believe in you, and besides,' I shrugged and gave her an encouraging smile, 'you get the chance to work on the ground. And from this day on, you will be on the ground, no more office work for you.' I turned and headed to my office.

It was true what I said about Sarah. She was good at what she did but lacked the confidence to stand on her feet. It reminded me of myself when I started. Mason had made sure that I built my confidence-fast! I had my first field work in a week after I joined in.

'There you are!' speaking of the devil, Mason was walking towards me, a smile on his face.

'Mmh,' I shook my head. 'That smile, Mason,' I pushed my door open and walked in. Placing my handbag on the desk I walked around it and started firing up my computers.

'No need for that today, Sky,' he said as he came in and perched on my desk. As usual, he was immaculately dressed in black slacks and a crisp white shirt, opened by the collar. In all the time that I have worked for him, I have only seen him wearing a tie three times, all those times he had no choice as his partner had forced him.

'What's up?' I pushed my chair back and looked at him.

'Alex Cadman called a few minutes before you got in,' he smiled, looking at his nails. 'I know he was supposed to come here for the meeting but he can't stay long. Today is the only day in his schedule that he has free to take you to see the place. So, he will be coming to pick you up from our front office in exactly,' he checked his time, 'five minutes. That said,' Mason stood up and placed his arms on his hips. 'You have the day off. Meet with him, go to the house, get the feel of it and start on your plans. I am sure after the tour; you'll want to go straight home.'

'And you tell me now?' I slumped on my chair. 'I should have been dressed for that!'

Mason took in my attire, a white dress with blue stripes. He raised an eyebrow at me, 'what is wrong with it?'

I tilted my head and put a leg forward. I was wearing heels, not really shoes that you would want to be walking around for long, 'see?'

'Mmh, I do see,' Mason placed his index finger on his lips. 'Figure something out; because,' he removed his phone and smiled, 'he is here. Hello, Alex,' he said as he took in my face. 'Oh, yes, yes. That will be fine. I have given her a day off so you can have her as long as you want. Yes, that will be alright.'

Now why did those words make me blush? I narrowed my eyes on him as I stood up and collected my small purse. I was not going to carry my two handbags the whole day! Removing my essentials, I placed them in the purse and closed it. I collected my car keys and stood back, waiting to hear what was being said.

Mason nodded to what Alex was saying, his eyes staying on my face. 'I will have someone drive her car to her house personally,' he held out his hand for my car keys.

I rolled my eyes and placed them on his palm. 'Seriously?'

'What?' Mason looked innocent. 'He says it's a three-hour drive from here. You check it out; probably have lunch there as well, before you turn back. How long will that be?'

'Why do I have a feeling that you are trying to hook us up?' I bit on my bottom lip.

'Sue me if I am,' Mason smiled as he escorted me through the door. 'Have fun.'

'I do have a boyfriend, you know,' I mumbled to him as he held the door open for me.

'I know,' he nodded. 'But you never know. He looked interested as well. It won't hurt to have a choice.'

I stopped by the door and smiled, 'you just sounded like my best friends right there!'

Mason winked at me and walked away. Taking a deep breath, I walked out towards the grey colored car that was parked in front of our offices.

Alex was standing outside, his eyes hidden behind of shades, making me thankful that I had my shades on as well. He stood up straight as I approached the vehicle.

'Miss Jamison, nice to see you again,' he held his hand out.

'Skyler, please,' I smiled as I took his outstretched hand. 'Nice to see you too, Alex,' I remembered he had given us a go ahead to use his name the day before.

'Are you ready?' he held the door open for me. 'We have a long drive ahead of us.'

I smiled as I slid into the car and waited for him to get in as well. I looked down at my feet once again and groaned. 'Uhm, is there any chance we could stop by a shoe shop?'

'Why?'

I could sense a frown behind his shades. 'My shoes are not fit to walk around for long,' I wiggled them to emphasize my meaning. 'I had thought we would just be meeting here for today.'

'You will be fine,' he said with a smile. 'Besides, I will be there to lend a hand if you need it.'

My breath caught in my throat, not because of the words he said, but in the way he said it. Turning to the side I watched as the landscape changed from the metropolitan that I was used to, to the lush greenery that was not so familiar to me.

'This will be my first time away from the city,' I found myself saying. 'The furthest I've ever been being a twenty minutes' drive on the opposite direction.'

Alex laughed, his voice sending shivers through my spine. It was low, sexy and full of confidence, 'then I am going to be your tour guide. I will point out all the great places I used to get into trouble in when I was younger.'

'You and trouble do not seem to go in the same sentence,' I gave him a smile, my shades hiding my eyes as I took his appearance in. He was not the drop dead gorgeous kind of guy, but the way he gave that side smile had me go weak in the knees. He had this attractiveness around him that I could not explain.

'Oh, believe me, I was trouble,' he nodded. 'The kind of guy mothers would warn their daughters against.'

'And now?'

He turned to me. I really wished he could remove his shades so that I look into his eyes. I squirmed a little on my seat. Even through those shades, I knew his gaze was checking me out. 'Now, I go for ladies who know what they want in life. Still a troublemaker, but in a different sense than before.'

'Meaning?' I could not help myself, I was curious.

'Meaning,' his voice went low, becoming deeper and husky. 'That if a woman knows what she wants, I do not mind. As long as our relationship is ours, we are free to do whatever we want.'

'Even if she has a boyfriend?' I just blurted out. I winced inward. Why couldn't I control my mouth!

He was quiet for a few seconds, his concentration on the road. A slow smile started breaking its way from his lips, 'I don't mind sharing,' he gave a slow shrug. 'Just as long as the other guy doesn't mind sharing as well. I like my relationships to be free of lies. If we are three or four in that relationship, that is the number. The moment I know that were are more than that, I am out.'

I frowned at him. He was so easy to talk to, so open. I found myself curious about him. 'So what you mean to say is that you are bisexual?'

A laugh so free escaped him. He shook his head in denial, still laughing. 'I might be adventurous but that is one path I will not be following. I have nothing against the people who choose that lifestyle, a handful of my friends do indeed live that way, with others completely homosexual. But that is not my cup of tea. I love women, to say it politely.'

I sat back and turned to the passing landscape. He made me think of things that I have never thought to think about. I had just met a man that satisfied me sexually as I have never been satisfied before. Jayden knew all the right buttons to press to get me where I wanted to be. He was gentle and considerate as a lover; a man I knew I was not going to be bored about.

But here was Alex, a very open sexual being who was not afraid to experience. A man who made me start to think about things that would never have crept in my head beforehand. Sighing, I closed my eyes. We still had about two hours and thirty minutes of driving to go, I might just as well close my eyes and sleep.

I was hot and needy, groaning as a pair of hands ran from my hips to just below my breasts. The person was behind me, I could not see who he was but I knew his touch, loved and craved it. His head lowered to the nape of my neck, tilting my head to the side to give him more space.

As he sucked on my neck, his thumbs flicked on my already hardened nipples. I groaned and tried to get his whole hand to take a hold of my breasts, which seemed to have grown heavy. I pushed back on him, coming in contact with his bulging front. My hand went behind and between us; I started rubbing him through his denim.

A small smile escaped me as I heard his hiss. This is why I loved him. He was not afraid to show me what he wanted and what he didn't.

'Kiss me,' I mumbled-gasped actually. I tried to turn but he stopped me, with his hands cupping my breast fully and pulling me deeper into his arms. 'Jayden,' I moaned. His lips were still playing havoc on my neck, my most sensitive part.

'No,' he whispered into my ear, his hands kneaded my breasts softly. 'We want you just like this.'

Even through my lust filled mind I frowned, 'what do you mean "we"?'

And that is when I felt a warm mouth taking one of my nipples into their mouths, and another pair of hands sliding between my thighs to the center of my being. I gasped a sound half sob and half moan escaped my lips as two fingers pressed on my clit. Who was this person? I opened my eyes, and looked down at the head on my breast. 'Alex?' I groaned as he sucked harder, rubbing me gently.

'Mmh,' he replied around my nipple. He gave it a little tug before turning his attention to the other one.

My feet felt weak from the double dose of stimulation that I was getting. One of my hands moved from rubbing on Jayden to Alex's shoulders as I tried to stay on my feet. 'W-what is going on?'

'Don't you like it?' Jayden asked from behind me. He removed my hand and undid his zipper. Reclaiming my hand, he placed it on his exposed member. 'Feel how hard I am for you.'

I groaned as I felt Alex's fingers penetrate me, the same time Jayden sucked on my neck. My world narrowed down to the two men and the sensations they were sending through my body.

'Do you think you can handle both of us, Sky?' Alex asked, his eyes holding mine. He had left the sucking of my tits to Jayden. He held my gaze with his blue one, his fingers entering and withdrawing from me. He picked up the tempo, making me grasp on him with both my hands, just to steady myself.

A low moan escaped me as I felt the quivering start in the pit of my stomach, rhythmical contractions of muscles. 'Alex, I am coming!' a slow scream started to build through me as I felt all the sensations in my body centered at one place. Jayden tugged at my breast with his teeth, before lapping it up and sucking it hard. The fingers between my legs increased their speed, the thumb pressing on my clit.

I threw my head back and let go, with a long and low scream.

I came awake with start. At first I was not sure where I was. Looking out the window, I noticed a few houses.

I frowned as I felt the last ⬚uivering leaving my body. What the hell? I was dreaming right? Does that mean I came for real? I glanced at Alex, his gaze was focused on the road. Clearing my throat, I sat up straight on my seat and smoothened down my dress.

'Good rest?'

A blush that I could not stop made its way up my cheeks, 'yes.' I was wondering how I am going to stop myself from looking at his fingers and recalling my dream the whole day.

Thinking that Alex's country was just that, a house, I was surprised to find a cottage. Not the traditional cottage with stone walls and thatched roof but a modern version of the cottages I was used to. Huge windows flanked the whole house, welcoming in the sunlight and nature. There was a huge stone fireplace, right in the middle of the lounge room. It was not such a big room but well decorated with shades of brown.

So, this is what I do when I want to have a feel of the room, I envision myself in that room, what I would like to do, how I would like things to look and flow around the room. I put myself in the house, and go through the motions as how people who own will do. When I am in this mode, everything and everyone seems to fade away.

I removed my shoes and walked to the soft leather chairs that were part of the furniture in the room. Sitting, I closed my eyes and tucked my feet under me. It might sound strange to people but that was how I worked. Time meant nothing to me when I was in this mode.

For the next hour or so I moved around the cottage, in the back of my mind I knew that Alex was following me. The cottage was beautiful, but I could see why they would want to redecorate. There were some places that were not easily accessible; some steps were just too steep.

'So,' Alex started as he took a seat opposite me. We were at an ice cream parlor, a stop that Alex had insisted on as we started making our way back to the city. 'Fancy some ice cream?'

I looked around me and smiled. 'You know this place reminds me of way back when my dad would sneak me out of the house and buy some ice cream for me. Mama was lactose intolerant, so nothing diary was allowed in the house. Too much temptation, she used to say,' I shook my head at the memory. 'But she used to keep éclairs for me. I would find them under my pillow once I got home from school.'

Alex was ⍰uiet for a few seconds, 'we could leave if this is uncomfortable,' he said softly.

I looked up at him and frowned, 'why would we do that?'

'Because I know both your parents have passed away,' he replied in the same soft voice. 'Mason told me,' he shrugged as a way of explaining.

I sat back and smiled, my arms crossing in front of me, 'and when, pray tell, did you and my boss sit and talk about me?'

He looked down, hiding the slight tint that was covering his cheeks.

I laughed, enjoying the slight discomfort that was evident on his face, 'and what else did my boss say about me?'

'Nothing much, actually,' he looked up, the arrogant tilt of his head back. 'He told me that if there was anything else that I wanted to know I should ask you.'

Before we could continue with our conversation, our waitress came through with our orders. Mine was a mix of strawberry, vanilla, mint and chocolate syrup. I looked up at Alex only to find him shaking his head. 'What?'

'That is one crazy mixture,' he replied as he took a sip from his chocolate milkshake.

I scooped some ice cream and placed it in my mouth, closing my eyes as my taste buds woke up. I have always tried different mixes with my ice cream, always going further and further. I opened my eyes and smiled, 'you should try it. It's heaven!' I took another mouthful and another. This was me. I am not the type of woman to deprive myself of something good just because there was a man around. I loved my ice cream and I did not care that Alex was there, or that he was watching me with fascination written on his face.

Without thought I took a spoonful of ice cream and extended it to him, 'would you like to have a taste?'

Alex gave me one of his lopsided smiles before taking hold of my hand and pulling it towards his mouth. As his lips closed around the spoon, his gaze held mine. He slowly removed the spoon, licking the remaining ice cream clean from it. His gaze was so hot, clashing with mine, not wanting to let go.

Trying to break the spell I dipped the spoon into my ice cream bowl and took a generous amount, hoping that it would quench the fire that was threatening to burn me alive.

'You have ice cream right here,' Alex drawled as he pointed to the side of his lips, for some reason his voice seemed deeper than usual. Not that I have known him that long but I knew there was a difference in his voice.

I licked the place he motioned, 'is it gone?'

He shook his head and leaned in, his eyes holding mine as his tongue darted out and licked on the side of my lips. I could not breath, it seemed as if I had forgotten how to. His tongue was so soft and it would have taken a mere inch of moving my head for our lips to touch. I watched him as he straightened back to his chair.

My hand went up and touched the place his tongue had been gently, 'why did you do that?'

He shrugged, 'I didn't want the tasty treat to go to waste.'

From the look in his eyes I was not sure if he was talking about the ice cream or a chance to taste my lips. Unconsciously, I licked my lips so that I could get rid of any that he missed.

'Has anyone ever told you that is a very provocative gesture?' his voice had grown deeper all of a sudden, and when I looked up I noticed his eyes were half open, as though he was trying to hide his thoughts from me.

'I am sorry?' I shook my head, trying to decipher what he might be talking about.

He gave me another one of his side smiles, 'licking your lips like that, very provocative. Makes a man want to do the honors, so to speak.'

I gasped as my fingers flew to my lips, a faint color covering my cheeks. Alex was proving to be too frank for comfort.

He laughed, 'you are precious!' He leaned forward and placed his hands on the table. Tilting his head sideways he smiled and shook his head, 'I am shocking you, aren't i?'

'A little,' I nodded. Why lie when he could probably see the shock written all over my face? 'I am not used to guys talking like that to me.'

He narrowed his eyes, 'but you are used to girls doing that?'

I smiled, 'yes. My two best friends are sexperts, if such a word exists. They will tell me all about what I should and should not do.'

'And do you listen to them?' he seemed intrigued, and who wouldn't? Sasha and Taylor were the craziest people in the world. Wherever we went, they left everlasting impressions, good or bad!

I laughed, 'nope. They usually have too many rules to remember and follow. I mostly do me.'

An eyebrow went up, 'not a fan of rules, are you?'

'Not really,' I scooped another spoonful of ice cream and placed it into my mouth, making sure that none was left on my lips. 'I do like to have them around, guide me in different situations, but I am not going to let them change who I am.'

He leaned back and smiled, 'interesting.'

Before I could ask him how so, my phone vibrated alerting me of a short message from Jayden. 'I am sorry,' I told him as started to read.

Just a reminder: No underwear allowed through the front door tonight

Jayden.

I could feel my cheeks turning beet red at the message. Placing the phone back on the table I reached for another scoop of ice cream, all of a sudden feeling a bit too hot.

Alex leaned forward and ran a thumb on one of my hot cheeks, 'you blush pretty,' he said as his eyes locked with mine. 'I wonder?'

I was mesmerized by the look in his eyes, so dominant and demanding, yet sexy and teasing at the same time. My temperature went up a notch, 'what is it that you were wondering?' Damn! Was that my voice? It sounded foreign even to my own ears-low and husky.

He leaned forward, his breath fanning my neck as he whispered in my ear, 'that is something for my fantasies. Or do you want to know about them?'

I could feel my eyes widening at that. This was so not unprofessional. He was a client for goodness sake and we were not supposed to be discussing anything else apart what should be done to the cottage. I swallowed hard, trying hard to calm my runaway heart. 'Uhm, no that won't be necessary.'

He laughed, low and sexy on my neck, 'chicken,' he said before he straightened up and looked at me. 'I better take you home before you expire of shock.' He reached for his wallet, took out a few bills and stood up. Holding his hand out, he coaxed his head to the side, watching for my reaction.

Taking a deep breath, I placed my hand on his and allowed him to pull me up. When I could have removed it from his grip he tightened on my hand.

We were about to walk out when a female voice called from the booth.

'Alexander Cadman!'

We both stopped and turned towards the voice. A woman of about thirty came towards us, her eyes undressing Alex.

'Oh no,' I heard Alex mumble under his breath as he plastered a smile on his face. 'Meredith Blay. Such a pleasant surprise to see you here.'

'I know, right!' Meredith threw herself into his arms, forcing a hug that Alex was really trying to get out of. 'Mmh, I missed you!' Meredith purred as she turned her gaze at me.

If it wasn't for the obvious discomfort that Alex was showing-his whole body had tensed up-I could have laughed. Instead, finding my inner actress, I glared at Meredith and cleared my throat. 'Baby?' I turned my gaze to Alex.

For a few seconds he looked confused, until it hit him that I was helping him. He disentangled himself from Meredith's python-like grip and moved to my side, placing his arm around my waist and pulling me in closer. 'Uhm-Mer let me introduce you to my girlfriend, Skyler.' He placed a kiss in my hair. 'Sky, Meredith and I grew up together. Same class until high school.'

I glanced back at Meredith noticing the color draining from her face. For a second, I felt kind of guilty. This was either Sasha or Taylor's territory, not mine. Taking in a deep breath I reached out my hand, 'hi!

CHAPTER 3

'Nice to meet someone who knew my darling when he was growing up! We should definitely find sometime and meet, so you can give me all the juicy stories,' I gave her a huge smile.

Meredith looked at my hand for a few seconds before she placed hers on mine. 'I am so sorry,' she looked flustered. 'Yeah, maybe some time.' She turned to Alex, 'it was nice seeing you again hey,' with that she walked away.

Alex did not wait but turned me around and dragged me outside. It was until we were in the safe zone of the car that I let my laugher bubble out of me. 'I am sorry,' I apologized when I saw his face clouding, but I just couldn't stop myself.

'Enjoying my discomfort, I see,' he said as he put the car into reverse.

'I thought you were invincible for a while,' I gasped for air as I chuckled, 'but one little woman had you ready to crawl under a rock!'

He glanced at me, 'Oh, Mer is not just a woman, she is a witch I tell you!' he shook his head. 'Once she gets her claws into you, she sinks them pretty deep.'

I doubled over, holding my stomach from so much laughing, 'whatever she did, I must really make truth of that meeting I told her about!' I wiped my eyes and chuckled. 'Why are we pulling over?' I asked with a big grin on my face.

He put the car into park before turning to me, his eyes dark. I saw some humor in them, before they clouded with an emotion I was not ready to decipher. 'I know one way to make you stop laughing.'

My breath hitched in my throat as my grin turned into a hesitant smile. I was not all together sure if I wanted to find out what it was that would make me stop laughing or that I already knew what he was about to do and welcomed it. 'And what is that?'

Alex reached out and took hold of my arm, gently but giving me no room to fight him he pulled me towards him, as he leaned forward. 'You are about to find out,' were words whispered on my lips before they were claimed by his.

Little electric shocks travelled from my lips to every part of my being, igniting a fire in my body that was not supposed to be there. I placed my hand on his chest, with all intentions of pushing him away but instead I took hold of his shirt and bunched it in my fist.

A groan escaped me as he deepened the kiss, his tongue seeking entrance to my mouth. I felt his hand travel upwards, until it reached the underside of my breast. His thumb made a swap on my now erect nipple, wringing a gasp from me which in turn gave his tongue access to mine.

What was happening? My foggy mind tried to bring me back to reality. With a groan I pushed him away, not knowing where the willpower came from.

He stopped the kiss, but did not let me go. Our eyes were still locked onto each other, our breaths a little rough.

'I-you,' I stammered as I shook my head. 'Why did you do that?' my voice was low, husky and confused.

'Second time you are asking me that question today, immediately after I have kissed you.' He flicked his thumb once again on my nipple, and nipped on my lower lip, 'found a way to make you stop laughing.' His voice gruff and low, making me think of dark nights, sweaty bodies and whispers in the dark. He searched my eyes with his, 'and also to find out if your groans and gasps are as sexy as your laugh. Now you have just piqued my interest even more.'

I felt my eyes widen. I was not going to act as though I did not understand his meaning, it was loud and clear, 'you want me in bed?'

He shook his head, 'I want your period. It can be on a bed, on a chair, table carpet,' he placed his other hand on my neck and pulled me closer. 'Fuck, it can be even in this car, I just want you.'

'I have a boyfriend,' I blurted out, thinking of anything that will make him back out. Though for some reason, way deep down that I did not want to reach, the thought of him backing out lased my heart with disappointment.

'As I told you before,' he gave me a lopsided smile, 'I don't mind sharing, so long as I know how many we are in a relationship.'

I frowned, 'that's not an answer. The question is how do you know Jayden doesn't mind sharing?'

'That is up to you to find out,' he placed a hard kiss on my lips before pulling back and putting the car back into drive. He turned to me, his eyes dark, heavy and full of desire that they robbed my breath away. 'Just get the answer fast, because if that kiss was any indication, I cannot wait to have you.'

I sat back into my chair, my whole body on full alert of the man sitting next to me. I stole a glance his way, just to make sure that he was serious and as if sensing my gaze, he turned to me, his eyes promising things that made my temperature rise. I groaned inwards, because truth be told I did want him too. But I also wanted Jayden and I did not want to do anything that would jeopardize our relationship.

What was I supposed to do?!

I laid in Jayden's arms that night, but my mind was not really fully there. And who could blame me, really? I had a gorgeous and attentive man with me, in bed with me, but I was thinking about the aggressive man who was not afraid to say what he wanted. I bunched my fist and bit down on a groan that was threatening to break free from my throat.

What was it Sasha told me when I called her earlier on? Ah, yes. Try all the goodies, might never know maybe you like a bit of both at the same time. I closed my eyes and tried not to shake my head.

Gazing up at Jayden's peaceful face I bit down on my lips. I did not want to lose him; I was already in love with him. But a part of me wanted to see what could come out between Alex and me.

Was I really contemplating starting something with Alex? My eyes widen. No! I moved tentatively so that I could not wake Jayden up. Placing his arm on his chest I wiggled out of the bed. Grabbing my silk robe, I covered my naked body and made my way downstairs. Sliding the glass doors open, I walked to the lounge chairs that Jayden had placed on his wooden deck behind the house.

I sighed heavily and rubbed my face, trying to scrub away what my mind wanted. My thoughts reverted back to the dream I had on our way to see that estate earlier that day. From a girl who did not date to a girl who fantasized about being with two men at the same time, what was wrong with me!

Rubbing my left shoulder, I looked up at the clear night sky, smiling at the stars and hoping to God that tomorrow I had the answers I really needed. It was either I refuse to work on Alex's house hence minimizing our interaction or working with him and constantly being in temptation mode.

'Hey,' Jayden's voice brought me back to the now.

I had been in deep thought that I did not hear him come out. I scooted a bit to give him space so he could fold his tall frame on my side. 'Hi,' I replied, my voice weak.

'Couldn't sleep?' he pushed a few strands of my hair away from my neck. He leaned down and placed a kiss on the crook of my neck while his other arm went to my waist, urging me to sit on his lap.

I did not fight him on this, crawling on his lap and burying my face on his chest. I shook my head as a reply to his question. 'Yeah.'

I could feel his fingers rubbing up and down on my bag, 'wanna talk about it?'

I moved so that I could look him in the eyes. He had concern written all over him, something that was eating at me. I traced his lips with my fingers, familiarizing myself with his features. 'Not yet,' I replied. 'I have to figure it out myself first.'

Jayden frowned, 'is it something to do with me? Are you not happy?'

'No!' I moved my legs on either side of him, straddling him and holding his face with my hands, 'it has nothing to do with you, Jayden. I love you! You make me feel treasured, loved, wanted and desired, things I did not think I would feel this fast with someone.'

Jayden took hold of my hand and placed a kiss on my palm. 'Will I get to hear about what is making you lose sleep anytime soon?'

I smiled, 'yes. For now, though,' I said as I placed my arms around him. I moved in for a kiss, stopping bare inches away. 'Right now I would love for you to fuck me. You owe it to me.'

Jayden laughed as he pulled me deeper into his arms, claiming my lips in a heart stopping, blood boiling kiss. 'Fucking is what you want, right?' he said between nips on my lips. His hands travelled from my hips to the small parting of my robe. His hands smoothed the panels open, exposing my already sensitive nipples to the cool air of the night, causing them to harden. He took hold of each of my tits in his hands, kneading and squeezing them in turn.

I groaned, as my tits were amongst my most sensitive anatomy. I moved my hands to his hair, running my fingers through his long strands of hair. 'Yes, that's what I want.'

He gave me one of his sexy grins before moving forward and claiming one of my nipples into his hot and wet mouth, while his remaining hand continued to massage my other tit. He continued to torture me with his ministration until I could not stay still on his lap, whimpering with suppressed desire.

'Stay still,' he whispered around my nipple.

'I can't,' I moaned as I arched my back, pushing my nipple deeper into his mouth.

He chuckled as he moved his attention to the other tit, his fingers taking over where his mouth had been. He went to work, his mouth tagging and licking on my nipples until I felt my blood boiling.

My hands went to his hair, pulling his face close to my bosom, holding him tight to where I wanted him. 'Jayden, stop teasing me already! I need this, I need you.'

The hand that Jayden had around my waist travelled to my front and dwelled between my open thighs, seeking my womanly flesh. His fingers skittered between my legs, coming to contact with my pulsing flesh.

'God, Jayden!' Without warning, an orgasm hit me hard, quivering around him as he held me in his arms until I caught my breath.

Without a word, he placed me on the lounge chair before standing up. He moved behind me, taking a hold on my waist as he went. For a few seconds we were standing face to face, before he turned me around. With a hand on my back, he slowly bent me over, bringing my behind flush to his front. I could feel his bulging front on my backside. He rubbed himself against me, wringing a small moan from my lips.

I pushed myself against him, telling him without words that I was ready for him. I kept my head lowered, my breath caught in my throat, the excitement of feeling him beside me turning my feet into gel.

I felt Jayden freeing himself from his pyjama bottoms and in a few seconds he entered me with a powerful thrust that had me tighten my hold on the lounge chair arm. A whimper escaped me, as he continued with his punishing movements. Not that I minded, I actually wanted him harder and faster. This is what I wanted. His hands moved from my waist and cupped my tits, squeezing them and pulling on the hardened nipples.

When I felt that I was closer to my second peak, I reached between our legs. Taking the sac between his legs in my hands, I gave them a gentle squeeze. I was rewarded with a groan and a tightening of his hands on my tits. Taking this as an encouragement, I continued to play with them, squeezing them between my hands, running my fingers on his shaft as it withdrew from me.

With two more powerful thrusts from him, I felt my vision clouding and my breathing coming out as a long and low scream as I came for the second time that night. I did not care if the neighbors were able to hear me, I could not control myself. Gasping, I continued to caress his sac as I came, wanting him to come with me. I was not disappointcd as I felt him stiffen behind me, before I felt a jet of warm li?uid inside me, triggering my third orgasm!

I was exhausted-good exhausted. I had collapsed on the lounge chair during the third orgasm, taking Jayden with me. When we had finally come down from the high, he had taken me back to the bedroom. After cleaning me and himself up, he joined me on the bed, taking me in his arms

'Are you alright?' he whispered on my hair.

I snuggled deeper into his arms, and sighed, 'I am more than alright.'

I walked into my office the next day, my decision already made. 'Is Mason in?'

Sarah was on her way to her own office, though she had been there before me that morning, 'yep. He was in very early today, actually.'

I frowned. The only time that Mason comes to the office early was when there was trouble in one of the sites or he had issues with his partner. Placing my bags down, I walked towards his office. My frown increased as I neared the door and heard laugher coming through. Sarah had not mentioned a meeting, and there was no sign on the door that stated a meeting was taking place.

Shrugging, I knocked, opening the door when I was bid to do so. I stopped in my tracks as I noticed Alex and Mason sitting on one of the sofas in Mason's office.

'Just the person we were talking about!' Mason stood up and walked towards me. he took my hand and pulled me to where Alex was also standing.

I arched an eyebrow at Mason, 'oh? What have I done?'

Mason laughed as he pushed me to sit down, 'nothing, darling.' He said as he sat opposite us. 'Alex was telling me about the house and how he watched you work.'

I blushed, 'oh. You know how I am, Mason. I hope it was not an inconvenience,' I turned to Alex.

Alex gave me a secret smile, 'not at all. It's very fascinating to watch you actually. You are so full of passion that is waiting to be revealed.'

I had a feeling that we were not talking about the same thing so I did the only thing I could do, ignore the comment. I turned to Mason, 'I had actually wanted to talk to you, but will come back later if you are busy.'

Alex stood up and shook his head, 'actually my business with Mason is done. I just came to invite you all to a party that I am throwing this Saturday.'

'We will be there,' Mason replied before I could say anything.

'I don't think I will be there,' I shook my head, my eyes on Mason as I noticed his frown. 'I already have an event to go to with my boyfriend on Saturday.' Jayden had told me that morning as I was preparing to come to work about a party a friend of his was holding that weekend. Apart from Travis and his workers, I really did not know most of Jayden's friends, and this was a chance to know some of them.

I could see the fallen looks on both Alex and Mason's faces, 'that is a shame,' Alex was ⬚uick to recover. 'Well, next time. When do I expect the concepts of what you are planning to do to the house?'

'About three weeks,' I replied with a nod.

Alex nodded and leaned forward, placing a kiss on the corner of my lips before shaking hands with Mason and leaving the office.

I turned to Mason, my eyes throwing daggers at him.

'What?' he asked in a bored tone as he moved to his desk. Sitting he turned on his computer and started acting busy.

I stood up and walked to his desk, placing my hands on the mahogany top, 'don't even think of acting busy, Mason! If it was any other client, you would have had a fit about what he just did right now!'

'No I wouldn't,' Mason shrugged, still not looking at me.

'Mason,' I groaned. 'I love you, I really do. But I would appreciate it if you do not play match maker with me. I have Jayden, I love him and I do not need anyone else trying to hook me up, damn it!'

This made him turn to me, 'I could have sworn that you have become so defensive all of a sudden, why is that?'

I pushed my short hair back, away from my face, 'I am not defensive, and I am just offended. I do not like to be pushed to someone,' I stopped him with my finger, 'and it's clear that is what you are doing. Anyway, the reason why I wanted to see you this morning is to tell you I cannot work on Cadman's house. Reasons being I am not comfortable with the whole situation.'

Mason narrowed his eyes, 'since when do you let your personal feeling into your work?'

'Since yesterday,' I sighed and sat down. 'Mason, I would never have asked you to take an account from me but Alex just makes me feel so-so,' I shrugged for the lack of works. I was not really sure how he made me feel and I really did not want to find out, it was a road I knew if I took will open doors that I was not sure I was ready to open at that time.

Mason sat back and finally looked at me straight in the eye, 'have you asked yourself why he makes you feel uncomfortable?'

I shrugged, it was my turn not to meet his eyes, 'it is something that I do not want to think about.'

'Mmh,' Mason sighed. 'Do you know how Simon and I met?'

I groaned. I knew that this was going to be a battle I was going to lose. He was not going to get the Cadman account off my hands. 'No, you never told me.'

'I was free out of design school when I landed a chance to decorate his late mother's house. He was also home from school at that time, he had a year to finish his architectural degree. From the word go he just made me uncomfortable, not in a bad way though. He seemed interested in all the steps I did, and of course he was not shy to show his interest in me.'

I could believe that! Simon was a straight forward person, who said what he meant at all times. Even though he was a silent partner but he made sure that his views were listened to when he aired them. 'But that's different.'

'I see the same fire in Alex towards you as I saw the fire in Simon towards me,' Mason nailed it in. 'I am not saying you should break it off with Jayden, I am sure you love him and so does he. I am just saying give Alex a chance. Getting to know someone does not mean you should sleep with them!'

The only thing I could do was just look at Mason. He had his mind made up so I had no choice but to go on with Cadman account. 'What you and Simon have is something unique, something special. It is something that I might have with Jayden, I do not want to ruin it. he makes me feel special, desired, wanted, loved, I can go on and on. Now you are pushing me towards Alex,' I stood up and shrugged. 'I don't want to lose Jayden, Mason. And if I do, because of this fixation you have about me and Alex, I will never forgive you.'

Mason smiled, not concerned with what I had said, 'never is a long time. You sure you cannot come on Saturday?'

I walked to the door, 'even if I could, I would not have come,' I gave him a smile and walked to my office. Sitting on my desk I swung it around so that I could face the window. I sighed and closed my eyes. So if plan A was not going to work I was to use plan B, been keeping my contact with Alex as minimal as possible. I would use the internet or text or phone calls for all correspondence, make sure that once the project starts I keep as far away from him as possible. This was going to work, wasn't it?

The fire that Mason had talked about was the same fire I felt with Jayden, but it was the same fire I felt with Alex-the ambers of it. These were tow completely different individuals. Where Jayden was playful and tactical, Alex was serious and straightforward. They were both demanding, but in different levels. And the crazy part was that they both made my heart feel as though I have been running a marathon!

I groaned. Turning my chair back towards my desk, I reached for my phone. Selecting Sasha and Taylor's numbers I quickly typed in a short message before sending it to them.

Help needed! This evening, my house. Wine and food on me!

I sat on the carpeted floor, a glass of wine in my hands. My two friends were currently looking at me as though I had two heads. And who could blame them? I mean, coming from a girl who had not dated for some time to someone who had two guys who clearly wanted her and not knowing what to do with the situation.

'Do not look at me like that,' I averted my eyes away from them.

Sasha snorted, 'how do you want us to look at you, sugar?' She shook her head and stood up. 'I need something stronger than this,' she placed her glass down and walked to my alcohol cabinet.

'But what do you want me to do, Sas?' I asked her as she walked back, sitting on the floor with me. 'You know how I am. I like Jayden, I really do,' I shook my head. 'But at the same time I find Alex interesting.'

Taylor reached down to take my left hand, 'I don't see a wedding ring right here, do you Sasha?' she showed my hand to Sasha who shook her head. 'Nor do I see an engagement ring. You are young, free and just started a relationship with Jayden. Not saying that it's not something great, it is. But you do have the right to see other people. You might never know, maybe it's Alex you might end up with.'

I groaned and placed my glass on the floor. 'Why is this happening to me?' I turned to my two friends. 'I was perfectly fine with Jayden, content. I was ready to give this whole relationship a chance, but now it's just complicating my life!'

'You are letting it complicate your life!' Taylor contradicted. 'Just let things run their course. If Alex wants you to have dinner with him, go ahead!'

'And if Jayden wants to have breakfast, go ahead,' Sasha took my right hand. 'Sky, you are too young to limit yourself right now. If you had been in a relationship with Jayden for more than six months, we wouldn't have said anything. But you are just getting to know the guy,' she ran her fingers through my hair, pushing it away from my face. 'No one is going to think badly of you for trying to find who you would love to see, date or have a relationship with.'

I smiled, 'I love you guys!' I am sorry, but I was feeling a little emotional. I just wanted someone to say loud what I was thinking inside my head.

'Aww, doll!' Taylor sat next to me on the floor and pulled me into her arms, 'we love you too! And whatever it is that you are going to choose we will be with you!'

Sasha placed a kiss on my lips, 'better believe it sugar,' she smiled. 'Now, I hate to be a sourpuss but I have to go. Landon is cooking for me tonight.' She was up and looking for her shoes.

'And we know how you love food,' Taylor snorted as she, too, stood up. 'I also have to go. Travis is taking me out for a movie.'

Sasha turned and pushed her hair back, 'of course! Black girl got to eat!'

'I just wonder where you put it all,' I teased as I stood up as well.

'No secret there!' Sasha walked to the door, her coat hanging over her arm while she grabbed her bag from the sofa. 'All the tussling on the bed does the work for me.'

Taylor collected her jacket and turned to me, 'see you tomorrow then? Travis told me about a party he and Jayden will be going to.'

'Yes,' I smiled. 'I will be there.'

Taylor reached out and hugged me, 'don't stress much. Everything will be fine.'

I kissed her and smiled, 'I won't.' At the skeptical look on her face I rolled my eyes, 'I promise.' With a final hug I watched her making her way to her car. Sasha was already pulling out of my drive way.

'You better not be thinking about backing out!' she called as she waved and drove off at a madwoman speed. Shaking my head, I blew a kiss at her, knowing that she will see it through her rearview mirror.

Taylor drove away at a much slower speed. I stood outside, watching my friends drive away before walking back into my house.

I collected my glass from the floor, taking sips as I cleared the remaining dishes. After finishing that, I walked to my bathroom. I quickly filled in the tub with warm water, adding my favorite bubble bath of magnolia. Lighting the scented candles, I collected my glass of wine and my phone. Placing them on the side stool, I quickly striped bcforc getting into the inviting water.

It was heavenly. My bathroom was where I liked to think, the only place I knew that I would be free from the stress of the world. I let the scent that filled the room seep into my stressed out muscles and relax them. Taking a sip from my glass, I settled back and closed my eyes.

It must have been about five minutes of silence when my phone started ringing. With a groan I reached out to it, 'hello? You telling me that you are at home already?'

'I have been home for a while, just wanted to know how you are,' a deep amused voice replied.

I sat up quickly in the bathtub as the voice registered. As I looked down, I saw my exposed breasts. With a gasp, I crossed my arm around my chest, only to groan when I realized he could not see me. 'Alex, uhm, hi!'

'Did I call you at a bad time?'

'Ye-I mean no,' I closed my eyes, trying to calm my nerves down. 'No, it's fine. I just wasn't expecting your call.'

'Clearly,' he responded. I could picture that smile of his playing on his face. 'You sound guilty, what are you doing?'

'Guilty?' I frowned. 'I am just-uhm-in my bathroom, taking a bath.'

I heard the squeaking of leather and I pictured him sitting back. 'Bathroom huh? Are you already naked? In the bath?'

'Well, I can't really take a bath with clothes, now can I?' I retorted. I closed my eyes trying to calm my body. Sweet Lord, just his voice had the power to make my lower muscles quiver.

He laughed. 'Touchy! How long have you been in there?'

'A few minutes,' I replied as I leaned back. I had decided I was going to answer his questions as short as possible so that he would leave me in peace.

'And are you comfortable?'

I rolled my eyes, 'I was.'

There was some silence for a few seconds, 'what has changed?'

Your cursed voice! 'You disturbed my calmness with your call. Why are you calling, Alex?'

'Just wanted to know how you were and if I could change your mind about tomorrow.'

'I am fine, thank you,' I said as politely as I could. 'And, no, I will not change my mind about tomorrow. I have already made a promise to my boyfriend.'

'Fair enough,' Alex agreed. 'Can you do me a favor?'

I swallowed. His voice had fallen another notch, making it deeper. 'What is it?'

'Can you run your hand from your neck to your breasts for me, slowly?'

'What?!' I sat up in the bathtub so fast that I dropped my glass into the tub and displaced some of the water.

'If I can't have you in real life, at least help me with my fantasies,' he said with a trace of humor and something else evident in his voice. 'You heard me. Do it, Sky, slowly.'

'You are insane!' I spat out. 'I can't do that!'

'Sure you can,' if possible his voice grew deeper. 'I am not even there to see it. Do it, Sky.'

All of a sudden my throath went dry. Could I really? He was not here; it wasn't as if he could see what I was doing! 'And when I am done?'

'We will move to more exciting areas of your body,' he replied. 'Do it, Skylar. Slowly, using only the tips of your fingers, run them down your neck to your breast, babe. Let me know how you feel.'

Taking a deep breath, I placed my fingers on my neck, slowly letting them follow the path to my breasts. I could feel the sensations right through to my toes. 'It feels nice,' I supplied when Alex asked me how it felt for the second time. Slowly I made my way to my breasts, the nipples wet from my bubble bath. As I drew closer to the nipple, it tightened. As I ran my finger on it, I had to gasp.

'Talk to me, Skylar,' he sounded hoarse.

'It,' I started before I had to close my eyes and concentrate. What did he ask? Oh yes. 'It's very sensitive. I feel it in the pits of my tummy,' I mumbled, hoping that he heard me.

'Take your whole breast in your hands, baby,' he commanded. 'Squeeze it for me, and imagine my lips on those perky nipples of yours. I would be sucking them hard, Sky. And as I suck on one, my hand will be playing with the other. Would you have liked that?'

I groaned as I closed my eyes. If it was possible to feel a person through the phone I could have said I just felt Alex's hot lips tugging on my nipples. 'Why are you doing this?'

He laughed, 'in order to get some sleep. One hand is on your other breast, my lips on your tight nipples, where do you want my other hand, Sky?'

On its own volition, my hand travelled south, to the quivering bud between my thighs. I gasped as my finger grazed the sensitive bud, crossing my legs over my hand. 'Alex!'

'Yes? Tell me what you did to gasp that way,' he coaxed me.

I blushed and shook my head. What was I doing? The last time I had phone sex was when I was in college, years back! But here I was sitting with my hand between my quivering thighs and a voice in my ear. I giggled, I could not help myself.

'Damn, that voice!' Alex groaned from the other side. 'Tell me, Sky. You are killing me!'

'You know where I would like your other hand to be,' I said softly. If he wanted to play this game, I would too. 'Right where it is right now,' I said as I uncrossed my legs, widening them a bit to give me more access to myself. I groaned loudly. 'That feels good!'

A sharp breath came through the phone, 'good girl! Now imagine me rubbing you down. My fingers going in circles around you, making you wetter than you are. Would you like that? Would you like my fingers to go lower still, closer and closer to that sensitive opening waiting for me to sink into?'

Oh, he was good! My fingers were working on the little bud, my lower muscles contracting from the sensations that I was giving myself. I closed my eyes and imagined Alex's fingers going lower, as my own fingers went lower. They circled the opening they found there. Even though with the water in the bathtub, I knew I was dripping wet. 'Yes,' I mumbled. 'Lower!'

'Good! Sink in a finger into that hole, baby and tell me how it feels! I want to know, Sky.'

My finger followed the instructions without hesitation. A long moan escaped me, my toes curling. Even though it was my finger but it felt foreign. I felt Alex's finger! 'Good God, Alex!'

'That's it, baby!' he mumbled. 'Now add another. Real slow,' he said.

I did, 'another moan escaped me.

'Now imagine me fucking you. My fingers going in and out, slowly at first then I increase the speed. Would you like that? Would you let me do that?'

My only answer was a gasp and a groan as my fingers took over and moved at the command of Alex's fantasies. They moved in and out, my breath coming out in gasps as pressure built inside of me. There was no more talk for me, just feelings that were building, tightening my muscles, curling up my toes. Out of nowhere an explosion started, shaking me to my core. 'Shit!' I said breathlessly as I threw my head back and rode my orgasm.

A low laugh brought me back, 'how was that?'

'That was something,' I replied breathlessly.

'I would love to see you cum, and taste you one of these days,' Alex said.

I closed my eyes and laughed. 'Good night, Alex.'

'Good night.'

I disconnected the phone and let it fall to the floor. I was spent and just wanted to enjoy the remnants of my orgasm. I licked my lips, thinking that I would have loved to see him cum as well. A small smile broke through my lips as I released the water in the bathtub. Oh yes, I would love to see him cum!

Saturday evening found me getting ready for Jayden's party. I had a relatively quiet morning and evening, with only Jayden calling me and reminding me of the time of the party and a trip to the salon to get my hair set for the evening. It was a little outside the city so we had to start off earlier. I had wanted him to come over, but he was tying up some business so we were only going to see each other that evening when he came to pick me up.

I sat in front of my dresser and stared at myself. My cheeks were flushed, eyes bright and all this was thanks to Alex and his phone episode. To say I was sexually frustrated would be putting it mildly! I groaned as I closed my eyes and ran my fingers through my short curls.

'Screw you, Alex!' I cursed as I took a deep breath to control myself. I really did not understand what was wrong with me, it's not as though I had been starving for sex. Hell, on the contrary I should have gained a whole lot of pounds for the sex I was getting! But what was it about Alex that made me feel hungry? 'Fuck it!' I stood up and started to dress up, having spied at the time.

I was just putting finishing touches on my makeup when my doorbell rang. Standing back, I smoothened the black dress down and looked myself over. Satisfied, I slipped my feet into my silver heels, collected my clutch bag and headed out.

I found Jayden leaning on the doorframe when I opened the door. I smiled as I heard his intake of breath. 'What?'

He stood up straight, looking gorgeous in his black shirt and black denim jeans. 'You look good,' he complimented me, his voice low and sexy. 'Might decide to change my mind and we spend the night in.'

'I don't mind,' I shrugged, blinking up at him. 'As long as you will be able to entertain me the whole night.'

He reached for me, pulling me into his arms before he buried his head on the crook of my neck, slowly kissing me. 'I can think of a few things we could do to keep each other entertained.'

A shiver went through my spine as I moved fully into his arms. 'Can you now?' my voice sounded husky even to my own ears.

Jayden nodded, a smile playing on his lips as they continue to torment me. 'Yes.' He groaned as he broke the kiss. 'But we have to go. It is important that I am present at this party as we are celebrating.' He looked me over, 'but we are not staying long!'

I laughed, 'promises, promises!'

I could see the regret in his eyes, and I knew that it was also reflecting on mine. Knowing that if I did not make a move we were going to stand there the whole night, I moved past him, walked to the car and waited for him to open the door for me. Today he was not driving his truck, but instead he was driving a sleek Audi R8 GT. 'Yours?' I asked.

He smiled as he opened the door, 'mine.'

I raised my eyebrow at him but got into the car. This was one expensive car; his job must really be paying that much. 'Cool ride.' I commented when he got in.

He threw back his head and laughed, 'yes, it is.'

'So how many cars do you have?' I never did venture to his garage when I was at his house. I knew he had a motorcycle; he had come to my house with it a few times.

'I have three,' he replied. 'The GMC, this one and I also have a GTO.'

'All manly cars, hey,' I smiled as my accountant-self started doing math in my head.

He smiled as he studied me for a few minutes before he shook his head and said, 'as you are doing your calculations make sure you indicate I have more than one source of income. Apart from the security company that I own, I am also a silent partner in two other very successful companies in the country or world, however you want to look at it. We are a group of four. Each of us has concentrated in what we are good at though we do support each other. The party we are going to is for one of our companies, actually.'

I was left with a wide opened mouth. Why didn't I see all this before? Because you interested in the man and not his money, I smiled to myself. 'How did you know I was doing calculations?'

'That little frown on your face,' he reached forward and ran a finger on my forehead. He let his finger trail down to my hand as he captured it. 'Regardless of the money, Sky, I am a simple man.'

I turned to him and smiled, 'I know and I think that is why I am attracted to him.'

'Only attracted?'

I swallowed hard. If I was honest with myself I would have told him that I loved him. But how could I say that when I had this issue with Alex hanging over my head. If I really loved Jayden, I shouldn't have been thinking of another man, right?

Seeing my conflict, he raised my hand to his lips, kissing it gently, 'one day at a time, Sky.'

The remaining drive was in relative silence, both enjoying each other's company without words. My interest piqued when we were driving through the gates of the house where the party was held. It was a grand house, very modern with more glass than block.

'Wow!'

'You should wait until you see the inside,' Jayden said as he switched off the ignition and got out. Going around the car, he opened the door for me and held my arm for assistance. 'Alex and I bought this house together; it's sort of our hide out when we want to get away from the world.'

I stumbled a bit at the mention of the name; thankfully Jayden's arm was around me. How many Alex's are there in the world? We cannot both know the same Alex. 'Alex?'

'Yeah, Alex Cadman,' Jayden supplied. 'He is a great friend and one of my silent partners. Travis is the other, who works for me at the security company and we have a lady by the name of Marsha.'

Oh Lord, give me strength! I felt like screaming, as I took a deep breath and walked up the stairs. Everything that I had tried to forget about the night before came back with a vengeance. I sniffled a groan and straightened my spine. Plastering a smile as Jayden opened the door, I was going through a dodge and hide plan in my head.

The room was already full, with people that I have only seen on newspapers and television. It was then that I figured out that Jayden was a rich man!

'Oh, you made it!' Taylor came through, a drink in her hands. 'Love the dress!'

I smiled as she hugged me, thankful that there was someone I knew at least. 'Looking good as well!' I turned to Travis as he made his way towards us. 'Hi, Travis,' I accepted his kiss on my cheek.

'Skyler,' he smiled as he turned to Jayden. 'I will have to steal you for a few minutes.'

Jayden looked at me, after nodding he placed a lingering kiss on my lips and left. I turned to Taylor, 'well, let's mingle!'

CHAPTER 4

Jayden's friends were great. I had my reservations at first, with them being big in the world of business, well known individuals, but after a few minutes they made me feel comfortable enough to chat with them. And all the time I was moving around, I was thankful that I did not run into Alex.

I had been wondering around the house, taking in the décor- occupational hazard- when I found myself outside. The gardens were vast and beautiful. There were spaces of darkness and places where lights shone bright. With a smile I walked down the cobbler stone, through a narrow walkway that led me down to the furthest side of the garden. With the moonlight I could make out a gazebo, well-hidden and empty, I headed there.

Just as I was about to step up the wooden stairs an arm snuck around my waist, pulling me back to a solid chest. I started to struggle when I figured out it was not Jayden's arms that were holding me back.

'Hold still!' the voice hissed. 'I am trying to control myself but you rubbing yourself on me is not making it easy!'

I sagged with relief, 'Alex!' I tried to turn and face him but his hands stopped me. 'What the hell do you think you are doing?' I gave up struggling and leaned into him.

'Holding you,' he replied, his lips on the crook of my neck, the exact same position Jayden's were earlier that evening. 'You smell good.'

'Alex,' I groaned as I tried again to break free, this time I succeeded. 'Stop it.'

He smiled and leaned on the wooden frame of the gazebo. 'I am not holding you-unless you want me to.'

I moved back one step, crossing my arms in front of me, 'why did you follow me here?'

'You and I have unfinished business,' he rubbed a finger on his jawline, his eyes studying me from head to toe. I could feel a faint blush covering my cheeks. He seemed to have noticed it as well as he gave me a lopsided smile, pushed himself away from the wooden frame and started to walk up the stairs and towards where I was standing.

'What business is that?' I tried to sound brave but my voice came out low and out of breath. I knew exactly what he was talking about.

He walked around me, his finger on my hand tracing patterns before he came and stood right in front of me. He placed a finger under my chin, forcing me to look up at him. 'You know exactly what it is.' He leaned forward, his lips mere inches from mine, 'but if you have forgotten I will enjoy the pleasure of reminding you.'

I groaned when his touched mine. I did not fight him off, what was the point? I wanted this, I wanted him. And if it was a kiss that I was going to get from him, I was not going to argue.

Noticing my surrender, Alex pulled me more fully into his arms, his lips coaxing mine in slow and seductive pulls. One of his arms went around my waist, pulling me closer to him while the other went to the side of my face, holding me still for his onslaught.

On their own volition, my hands went between us, bunching the white shirt that he was wearing. Oh, his kiss was making me weak. At that moment Jayden was far from my mind, it was all about Alex. One of my hands moved to his neck, pulling closer and deepening the kiss.

Alex took his time; he did not rush. He took his time deepening the kiss, all the time he was in control of it.

I became bolder, running my hand on his chest as the fingers of my other hand weaved through his hair. I guess that was what he was waiting for as he became more demanding, deepening the kiss. I could feel myself becoming lightheaded.

Alex's lips left my lips and travelled to my neck, his hand tracing the low V in front of my dress, 'you do know how to tease a man, Skyler.'

'Wh-what?' I gasped as his hand cupped on of my breasts, his finger flicking the nipple.

'This dress,' he moved back and looked down at me. 'The only thing I could think of was removing it from you. All this skin,' he moved his finger to the sleeve of my dress, moving it so that my shoulder was naked. Alex leaned in and placed a kiss on my shoulder as the other hand that was on my waist, slowly traveled south, until it reached the slit in front of my dress. His hand then started traveling upward, taking my dress with it.

I looked around and at that moment I thought of Jayden. What was I doing?! 'Wait!' I gasped as his finger came into contact with my already wet core. Groaning, I rested my head on his shoulder. 'We can't.'

'Why not?'

I looked up at him, 'Jayden.' I squirmed when his finger again flicked on my clit, biting my lip to stop from shouting out.

Alex looked over my shoulder for a second before a smile broke down on his lips, 'he doesn't mind.' He leaned forward again, taking my lips in a hard sensual kiss that left me shaking to my shoes. With the kiss robbing me of my senses I let myself go, enjoying what his fingers were doing to me.

'I want to taste you,' he whispered as he moved me backwards until I sat on one of the wooden benches that furnished the gazebo. Alex did not waste time, he went on his knees in front of me. All I could do was watch as he removed my panties before stuffing them into his pockets. His hands then went to my thighs, smoothing them up as he took my dress with him. In a few minutes I sat there, exposed to him and his ministrations.

'I did tell you that I wanted to taste you,' he mumbled as he placed a kiss on my inner thigh, just inches from my clit. I groaned as I felt it quiver, wanting his touch, his tongue there.

I closed my eyes and held my breath, waiting, panting for his tongue. When it finally reached where I wanted it the most, I could not stop the low moan that escaped me. Oh it felt good!

Alex knew exactly what he was doing, moving his tongue on my aroused bud in slow licks, his tongue circling the opening of my channel before his lips closed tightly around my mound and sucked hard.

I gasped, feeling the tightening of my muscles which indicated I was about to come. Alex was in tune with my body, licking and sucking me harder and faster as the tension built up inside me. Placing my hand on his head, I pulled him to me as my breathing ceased. A low groan and a shudder warned him of my orgasm. He gave me a good hard suck before lapping on my cum juices, sending small shivers through my still trembling body.

'Are you ok?' he asked as he moved up and placed a gentle kiss on my lips, his eyes questioning.

I sighed as I tried to sit up, licking my dry lips and smiling as his eyes darkened. I knew exactly what I was doing to him, tasting myself on my lips from his kiss. 'Yes. I am perfect.'

He grinned and looked over his shoulder. I frowned as I followed his gaze, fear that maybe I shouted when I was coming and had the whole house watching us. My mouth fell open when my eyes came into contact with Jayden's.

To make things worse, he had the same smile as the one Alex had at the moment, a very satisfied smile.
I could not believe that Jayden had been watching us the whole time nor that Alex had known that he was there and still continued to give me pleasure. I frowned at the thought, my eyes narrowing as I looked from one face to the other. They looked so pleased.

'What's going on here?' I stood up, pulling my dress down as I did. 'Aren't you supposed to be angry or something?' My frown deepened as I looked at Jayden. He had abandoned his position by the gazebo entrance and was now slowly walking to where Alex and I were standing.

He shrugged, 'why should I be?'

'Why should you be?' I repeated slowly. 'You are asking why you should be angry? Your friend, partner-whatever just tongued me to orgasm and you are asking me why you should be angry?'

Jayden stopped in front of me and shook his head. 'The only reason I am angry is that you started before me,' he ran his thumb across my still swollen lips. 'I would have liked it better if I was here from the beginning.'

My mind riled. What was he really saying? He didn't mind someone else made me come? I pushed his hand away from my lips, moved away from him. 'What?'

Alex sighed, the first sound from him since Jayden and I started talking. Moving to my side, he placed his arm around my shoulders, pulling me to him. 'There is something that you need to know about Jayden and me.'

My eyes widened at that statement, 'are you gay? And you thought of using me to make each other jealous?' I could feel my body vibrating with fury.

Jayden shook his head, 'no, neither are we bisexual.'

'But the relationships that we have are not the traditional ones of boy and girl,' Alex explained. 'Look, we both wanted you and now we have you.'

I pushed him away from me, using so much force that he had to take a step back. 'Are you both insane? What? Did you sit down one day and thought maybe you'd just find an unexpected girl and share her between the two of you just for fun?'

'Sky,' Jayden started.

I turned to him, my eyes spitting fire at him, 'don't you "Sky" me! How could you?' I shook my head, fighting down the tears that were threatening to fall. Shaking my head, I moved away from them. 'I need to get out of here.' I turned and started walking away before Jayden's hand stopped me.

'Baby, wait.'

Shaking his hand off I walked away as fast as my heels could allow me.

Re-entering the party, I scanned the room, making a beeline straight to Taylor when I located her.

'I have to get out of here,' was the only thing I could say when I reached her side.

Thankfully she did not ask me anything. Taking my hand, she led me to the front door, 'Travis had said there is a cab service for tonight. We can get you one.'

I nodded and followed her. True to her words we found about four cabs packed outside. Getting to one, I looked up at Taylor, her worry showing on her face. 'I will call you,' I told her.

'You do that,' she leaned in and kissed me.

The main door opened, bringing Jayden and Alex into view. 'Let's go,' I told the cab driver as I watched the two men come down the stairs. I could hear them calling my name but I ignored, instead I told the cab driver to go fast.

I sat back on the back seat and closed my eyes, trying hard to fight the tears that were threatening to fall. This is what I get for not being able to make up my mind, I thought to myself.

'Are you ok?'

My eyes flew open, clashing with those of the cab driver on his rear-view mirror.

I tried to smile but failed, instead I just nodded my head, turning it away from the sympathetic look he gave me.

My phone started ringing. Taking it from my clutch bag I looked at it for a while before rejecting the call. I wanted to turn it off but I couldn't because I knew Taylor would call soon. Instead I placed the phone on silent, placing it back into my bag.

Getting home, I ⬛uickly paid the driver, before running up my driveway. After two attempts on opening my front door, I let myself into my house. Leaning on the door I closed my eyes and took a deep breath. This was stupid. I was stupid. Why was I upset about the whole thing? It was Jayden who was entitled to be upset; we were in a relationship for goodness sake! But he seemed cool with it. And I guess that's what unsettled me the most.

Taking my phone from my bag I groaned. 15 missed calls from Jayden and Alex, 2 voice messages and 6 short messages. Kicking my shoes off, I dialed Taylor's number, ignoring the rest. 'Am home,' I said when we were connected.

'Good,' she sighed with relief. 'They got out of here a few minutes ago. Whatever happened?'

'I'll tell you tomorrow. I am still raw about it. Good night.'

'Night, doll. We will come tomorrow, Sasha and I.' she hung up.

Just as I was about to head to my room there was consistent knocking on my door, and I knew exactly who it was.

'We know you are in there,' Jayden called. 'Come on, baby, open the door!'

I stood still, not even breathing.

'Sky, we need to talk about this,' came Alex's voice.

I took a deep breath, 'you had better get off my property right now before I call the police!'

'Baby, it's not what you think; please let us talk to you.' Jayden pleaded.

'Not what I think?' I screeched, my legs moving towards the door. 'You have no idea what I am thinking right now! Just leave, now!'

'We know you are upset and we understand,' Alex stepped in. 'We should have told you from the start, and that's our mistake. But we would like to talk to you now.'

'But I don't want to talk to you,' I replied, my voice thick with emotion. 'I don't think I want to talk to you both ever.'

'Baby,' Jayden coaxed.

'Please,' I begged as tears started falling. 'Please just leave. I c-can't deal with this right now.'

There were a few curses, a slap on the wall and deep breaths before I heard footsteps walk away from my door.

Sagging to the floor, I let the tears fall.

The following day found me curled up on my sofa, a glass of wine in my hand and two friends staring at me as though I had just grown horns.

'Mind telling me that story again?' Sasha enquired.

Taylor rolled her eyes, 'she told it to you a dozen times! Seriously, Sash.'

I looked at the two of them and tried to smile.

'What are you going to do?' Taylor asked, her eyes sparkling.

I shrugged. I really did not know what I was going to do. My mind was still jumbled up. 'At the moment I just do not want to talk to either of them.'

'You will have to,' Sasha glanced at the blinking light on my land line.

I closed my eyes and shook my head, 'not at this moment.'

The remainder of the weekend dragged by and so did the week ahead. I found every excuse to be out of the office, just in case Alex decided to show up at the office. Mason tried to coax information about what happened but I felt ashamed and did not tell him anything. How could I just open my legs to Alex so fast? Every time I think about it my emotions change. By Friday my emotions ranged from anger to confusion to downright turn on.

'You know what you need?' Sasha said around a spoon of ice cream. We were seated at our favorite restaurant eating lunch.

'A spanking?' I grunted.

'I am sure Alex or Jayden won't mind giving that to you. But no, I am talking about going out and letting your hair down and your frustrations as well. Tonight. My treat.'

'I'm in,' Taylor clapped. 'You need this, Sky.'

I rolled my eyes, 'do I have a choice?'

'No!' A unison denial echoed.

So now here I was seated at the bar, nursing my chili margarita. My friends as usual were on the dance floor, doing their thing. Those two could dance the night away. I needed refilling. I turned and looked at them, smiling as they waved for me to join them. Downing the drink, I joined them on the floor, letting all the frustrations go.

'I'm heading to the loo!' I screamed on top of the music after four songs. 'Those drinks are playing havoc on my bladder!'

I made my way off the dance floor, continuously humming and bobbing my head to the song. As I finally made it off the floor, I turned to head to the lady's room, only for my hand to be snagged and pulled to the other direction.

'What the he-,' I looked up and came face to face with Jayden. 'Jayden, wh-?'

Before I could finish my question his lips captured mine in a kiss that had me breathless in a second. On its own volition my hand slid up and touched his cheek. Too soon he broke the kiss, but trailed his lips down my jawline to my ear.

'Come with me,' he whispered before straightening and holding my hand.

I was powerless to stop myself from following him, not that I wanted to.

He led me to the VIP section, where people could sit and watch people without being seen. The cubicles were designed with their own doors, decorated with leather sofas, private bars and toilets. We walked to the cubicle that was furthest from the rest. For some reason my heart was beating a bit too fast, butterflies were taking flight in my tummy.

When we got to the last cubicle, he stopped, pulled me back into his arms and kissed me again. His hands were on my hips, holding me so close that I could feel the bulge on the front of his trousers. Groaning I moved myself even closer to him.

'We want to show you something,' he whispered against my lips, claiming it when I was about to voice out my question.

He did say we, didn't he? I asked myself as I felt myself being forward.

Jayden pulled me into the dim lit cubicle. There was soft music playing in the background, flames from the candles casting shadows but my eyes were on the other man in the room.

'What's going on?' I whispered as my eyes swung from Jayden to Alex, the flutter in my tummy increasing.

Jayden moved behind me, his arm going around my waist as he pulled me back to him. He trailed kisses from my cheek to my neck and shoulder before going back to my neck. He flicked his tongue on my skin, wringing out a shudder from me that had his arm tightening. All this while Alex was just watching us, his gaze intense that I felt my skin growing hot.

Jayden's other hand went under the top I was wearing, travelled up my waist and stopped right under my breast which was braless.

I could not stop the groan that escaped me when his thumb flickered on my already hardened and sensitive nipples. Closing my eyes, I pushed my breast on his hand, wanting more of his touch.

'Open your eyes,' the hoarse command was from Jayden. 'Keep them on Alex.'

I obeyed, hazel eyes clashing with blue. Alex gave me his lopsided smile, his eyes darkening when I bit on my lower lip to stop from moaning out loud.

Jayden was still teasing my nipple; I could feel each stroke of his thumb down my womb. Moving my thighs, I tried to stimulate myself, groaning with frustration. 'Jayden,' I moaned, with my eyes still on Alex. A flush of color tinted my cheeks as I remembered what his tongue and mouth did to me.

'Shh,' Jayden hushed me. He moved the hand that was on my waist to the front of the shorts I was wearing. Sneaking it in, he ran his finger on the top of the lacy panties I was wearing.

'Lower,' I ordered-pleaded.

My eyes widened when Alex stood up from his position and made his way to where we were standing. He stopped in front of me, his hand going up to push my hair back. With his eyes locked with mine he leaned forward and claimed my lips in a coaxing kiss. I groaned deep. I had two lips on my neck that were driving me crazy, a hand on my nipple and another below my belly button. Jayden's hand moved back up, claiming my other breast while Alex's hand took the place below my shorts. His seeking fingers traced the outline of my panties before going even lower and touching me there, where the bud was tight and sensitive and seeking fulfilment. He ran a finger gently on my clit, groaning as he did so.

'You are already wet,' he smiled on my lips.

I was thankful for the low lighting in the room as another blush covered me.

Pushing my panties aside, Alex came into contact with my clit, rubbing it gently and in circles. I could not help myself, my hips grinded on his finger. At that same time Jayden cupped my breasts fully. He took a hold of my nipples between his thumbs and index fingers, rubbing them gently before pulling at them.

'Shit!' I breathed, as I had to lean on Alex for support.

'We got you,' Alex mumbled as he took my lips in another kiss, the same time two of his fingers sank into my wet core.

The quad stimulation that I was getting from two lips and four hands at the same time was too much. The pressure in my womb grew so fast and quick that I had no choice but to let it out.

With a gasp, which was swallowed by Alex, I let go, coming so hard that the only thing that kept me from sinking to the ground was Alex's arm around my waist. His fingers continued pistoling into me, as Jayden's hands continued to torture my nipples. To my own shock I came again, with a low moan that went on forever!

Slowly the two men started to withdraw. Jayden let go of my nipples, his hands circling my waist, while Alex withdrew from inside me, bringing his fingers to his lips and licking my juices off them.

I could not walk to save myself so I let them lead me to the single sofa in the room. With each man on one side, they attacked my senses once again, kissing me down my neck on either side. Alex's hand went to my waist, pulling my top to my neck, releasing my breasts to them.

'No bra?' Alex asked as his tongue snaked around one of my nipples.

'I'm not complaining,' Jayden mumbled against the other.

The sucking and pulling of my nipples by the two men had me hot and bothered. My hands went to their thighs, rubbing them up and down. But as I moved them up, two hands stopped me at the same time.

'But-,' I started as I wiggled my hands to get them free.

'No,' Jayden shook his head. He bent down, took my nipple into his hot mouth and sucked hard before he released it and stood up.

Alex bit around my breast, flicked his tongue on my nipple before he, too, stood up. They stood there looking at me, his eyes hooded. 'We have just given you a taste of how it could be with us. We both want you,' Alex said, seriously.

'But it is up to you,' Jayden added. 'We come together, Sky. It's not him or I, it's us. The ball is in your corner now, sweetheart.' Jayden turned and walked to the door.

'You know where we are,' Alex added. 'When you make up your mind, come and find us.'

I watched as they walked out of the room, leaving me there panting and so aroused it was close to pain. Groaning, I closed my eyes and pushed my hair away from my face.

I sat there staring at my computer screen for what seemed to be hours. I was supposed to be working on the plans for Alex's project, but just the thought of that man made my skin flush-crawl at the same time. It was a Thursday, six days after their tease-torture routine at the club. I had been ignoring them both, not that they had called or anything. They were keeping to their promise, that if I wanted them, I should go to them as I knew where they would be. And I did know, but my pride wouldn't let me follow them.

'Sky?' Harris poked his head into my office.

'WHAT!' I barked before I could stop myself. Sexual frustration could make any girl crazy. Taking a deep breath, I closed my eyes and counted to ten. When I finally opened them I focused on the man with his hand on the door and eyes as big as saucers. 'Please forgive me, Harris. I have a lot on my mind.'

Harris looked me over for a few seconds.

I rolled my eyes and waved him in, 'it's not like I have sprout devil horns or anything.

'Is this that time of the month?' he asked cautiously as he sat opposite me.

'Ha ha ha, very funny! Why do you guys think it's all about the red polka dot?' I tilted my head, bursting into a laugh when I saw his uncomfortable face, 'never mind. That is not what brought you here.'

'Definitely not,' he shook his head vigorously.

'So?' I intertwined my fingers on my desk and looked all professional 'What can I do for you?'

'My girlfriend and I are planning to move in together...,' he frowned. 'What?'

I noticed that my mouth was open. Closing it quickly I shook my head. 'I didn't know you were seeing someone, that's all.'

He blushed, 'for six months now,' he said proudly

Where have I been all these six months? I asked myself as I kept a smile on my face. 'Congrats. So what do you need from me?'

'Tips on how to change my bachelor pad into something decent for a woman.'

I smiled. 'Well, you have come to the right person!' Instead of working on Alex's project I stared with Harris. It was something that was keeping me from him-them. How do I tell them what I felt? For both of them? I had come to realize that my fighting the feelings was actually working against me.

'I have to tell them,' I mumbled to myself as I watched Harris leave my office. 'On Saturday I will go to their house and talk to them both.'

Saturday night found me sitting in my car, parked on the driveway of Alex's and Jayden's getaway house. I was still debating with myself as to whether I should climb the stairs leading to the main house or just turn my car around and drive back home. I looked up at the house. There were lights in on the foyer and one of the rooms upstairs. Gripping my steering wheel, I closed my eyes, called for strength and opened my door. Walking as fast as I could, I rang the bell before I could change my mind.

It felt like forever waiting for the door to open. My nerves were so tight and my hands clammy. Was I really going to do this? Without thought I started to move away from the door, one step back before I realized what I was doing. Taking a deep breath, I rubbed my clammy hands on the soft skirt that I had on and squared my shoulders.

A gasp escaped me when finally, the door swung open and Alex stood there, with only his cream linen trousers. I could feel butterflies taking flight in my tummy and I swallowed hard to moisten my suddenly dry throat.

Alex frowned a little when he looked at me. He tilted his head to the side, trying to see more of my expression before he stood to the side and allowed me entrance.

I had no idea how my legs moved, as they felt like lead at that moment. I walked in, passed him into the familiar hallway. Reaching the middle, I stopped and turned to him. He was leaning on the door and studying me, making me so self-conscious that I started to blush.

'Yo, Alex, who's at the door?' Jayden called from a room that was closed the night of the party. There was some shuffling and then the door was pushed further open and out came Jayden. He was dressed in black surfer shorts and a matching tank-top. His eyes narrowed when they landed on me. He turned to Alex, and from the corner of my eyes I could see his shrug.

Taking a deep breath, I smiled a little, 'can we sit and talk?' When I saw none of them making a move, I sighed, 'please?'

'The lounge is good enough a place,' Jayden led the way.

Alex was about to follow when I stopped him, 'please put something on before we talk. You are very-uhm-distracting,' I blushed further as he walked passed me, making sure he was close enough for contact.

Jayden stood on the side of the entryway, waiting for me to precede him. There was no backing down now, I thought to myself as I walked in and chose the only one sitter in the room.

'Can I get you something to drink?' Jayden asked as he fixed himself a whiskey.

'No, thank you,' I declined. I wanted a clear head about this.

Jayden shrugged and took two glasses to the two sitter that was facing me. He sat back, one hand nursing his drink while the other resting on the back of the sofa, his eyes roaming on my face. A few seconds later Alex walked in. He took his seat next to Jayden and reached for his drink.

With the two pairs of eyes both trained on me, power of speech deserted me. I shook my head and looked at them. These two were total opposites of each other, even the way they sat, they talked or even dressed. And I wanted them both.

Then tell them! I shouted at myself.

'I can see the wheels in your head turning, lioness,' Jayden mumbled as he swung his drink around his glass. 'Want to share your thought?'

'I don't know where to begin,' I replied truthfully.

Alex sat back, he stared into his drink for a few seconds, took a sip before looking straight at me. 'How about starting with why you are here?'

My tongue snuck out and moistened my dry lips. I could see that was the wrong-or right thing to do as the two pairs of eyes darkened at the same time. 'I wanted to know.....' I stopped. What did I want to know? I asked myself.

'What did you want to know, lioness?' Jayden drawled, his gaze fixed on my lips.

I shook my head. The gazes that they were giving me were making me hot. Uncrossing my knees, I wiped my hands on the skirt I was wearing. 'I am not sure.'

Alex gave me a lopsided smile before placing his drink down and standing up. I watched him with fascination as he walked slowly towards me. I scooted a bit when he sat on the arm chair of my seat. He placed his hand at the back of my seat, his fingers brushing softly on my covered shoulder.

'Are you sure that you do not know?' he leaned forward and whispered into my ear.

I shiver ran through my body. This was not going according to my plans, I thought. Alex's hand moved on my shoulder and pulled me even closer towards him. 'I-I think I was curious. You had said that if I wanted one I have to get the other. H-how does that work?' I asked, the hand distracting me.

'It's very simple,' Jayden stood up and walked to the other side of my seat. He did the same thing as what Alex had done. There I was, caged between the two men that I found irresistible. 'You and us, in a relationship. It will be like any other relationship but you will have both of us.'

'B-both of you?' I gulped. 'How would that work?'

Jayden pushed a strand of hair away from my face, his finger travelling down my cheek to rest on my chin. With little pressure he forced me to look at him. I watched as his face descends towards mine. My lips parted just before his touched mine. His lips slowly moved against mine, gentle as butterfly wings but I still felt it on my toes.

As Jayden continued to gently kiss me, I felt Alex move closer. In a few seconds I felt his lips on my neck, as gentle as Jayden. I closed my eyes as I tried to concentrate on the double dose of sensations. As one of Alex's hand continued to touch my shoulder, I felt his other hand resting on my thigh. I could feel it moving up, taking my mini skirt with it.

As Alex's hand worked on my thighs, Jayden's started to work on my chest. His hand crept inside my vest, pulling it free from the skirt. I gasped as I felt his cool fingers travelling up, taking my top with him. I groaned as I felt Jayden's hands lightly brushed the underside of my breast.

I felt a smile on his lips, 'no bra again, lioness?'

I blushed, 'uhm-the top has padding,' I explained.

Alex chuckled as he reached where his seeking hands were moving to, 'no panties as well,' he mumbled against my neck. He placed a kiss before moving back and studying me.

I felt self-conscious as both men stared down at me. I squirmed a little as Alex's finger found my wet suit.

'Did you do this on purpose, Sky?' Alex asked as his finger slid through my wet folds. I gasped as one of his fingers made its way into me. 'And you are so wet.'

Jayden's fingers flicked on my already hardened nipple, 'you have not answered the question, lioness. Did you come without your panties and bra on purpose?'

I bit down on a groan. The combination of Alex's finger as well as Jayden's was making me crazy with want. I moved my hips, trying to get Alex's finger deeper into me. As if knowing my intentions, Alex moved his finger out. He circled his finger on my opening. 'Sky?'

'Yes!' I gasped.

'Why?' Jayden asked as he rubbed my nipple between his fingers.

I moaned, 'because I wanted to seduce you both and I didn't know what to do.' I confessed. I got up so fast that they had no chance of catching me. Placing my hands on my hips I shook my head, 'I don't think I can stop myself from wanting you.'

The two men stood up at the same time, made their way towards me. Jayden got there first, framing my face with his hands. 'We can't stop wanting you too, lioness. It's not like we do not understand how this may look to you, but we want to be with you, both of us.'

'We will go as slow as you want us to,' Alex chipped in. 'You control this.'

Jayden pulled me into his arms, 'we might act as though we are the ones running the show, but it's all you, baby.'

Alex moved behind me, his arms going around me from there, 'you have so much control over us, Sky, don't you ever forget that.'

I felt safe in their arms, wanted, cherished and all those feelings that all girls would love to feel. I sighed, placing a hand around Jayden's waist as I placed the other on Alex's arm. 'I don't think I want to go slow tonight. I need you, both of you and it's just driving me crazy!'

'We got you,' Jayden whispered as I felt his lips on the right hand side of my neck. Alex pulled me back against him. With my arm still around Jayden, we moved together.

A giggle escaped me, 'make love to me, you two!'

And that is what they proceeded to do. I have no clear recollection as to how we moved from the lounge to one of the bedrooms. All that was filled in my head were Jayden's lips and hands, followed by Alex's hands and lips. There was no inch of my skin that was left untouched by the two men, they were that thorough.

'I want to taste you,' Alex groaned on my tummy. I was lying face up with Alex between my legs and Jayden just above my head. I had been stroking and suckling on Jayden's hardened member as Alex travelled down my body.

I looked over at him and smiled, 'addicted, aren't you?' I teased him as I stole a lick from Jayden's member.

'You have no idea,' Alex's eyes glazed over as he gently ran his tongue over my drenched folds. I could not help myself, arching my back to push myself deeper into his mouth. I took Jayden back into my mouth, sucking him to the rhythm of Alex's licking.

'Lioness!' Jayden groaned as he took a hold of my hair and forced me to take more of him inside my mouth.

I moved back, causing the head of his pulsing member to be sucked out of my mouth. 'Tell Alex to let me cum and I will give you your release,' I told him through gritted teeth as I felt Alex's tongue enter my opening. I took Jayden back in, still mimicking the way Alex was pleasuring me.

'Alex,' Jayden breathed out, 'I am dying here.'

With that Alex went hard to work. He sucked, nipped and licked until all I could think about was his tongue. Increasing my tempo, I also sucked on Jayden, giving some attention to the sac between his thighs as well. I sucked him hard, wringing out a gasp and a groan from him.

All of a sudden my eyes rolled back as an orgasm so hard hit me. Giving Jayden a final suck I released him with a pop as I surfed on my orgasm. Before I could catch my breath I was pulled above Jayden, who was now laying on the bed. Straddling him, it brought my opening in contact with his hard manhood. A simultaneous groan escaped us and I bent lower to claim his lips.

'Are you ready for me, baby?' his voice was strained, hoarse and low.

Words had escaped me so I just nodded, groaning out loudly when he entered me. With sure strokes, Jayden drove into me, each time a gasp escaped me. For a while it was just me and Jayden, until I felt a warm hand caressing my butt cheeks. Alex was massaging them gently, running a finger through my crack and rubbing on the tight hole there.

I moved forward, not sure about the anal thing. Not that I did not know anything about it, no. The reason was that I had tried it before and I just felt pain and no pleasure. I swung my head back, looking at Alex. 'I-I'm not so sure about that.' I moaned as his finger pressed into me gently. I felt a cool liquid being pushed in as well.

'Relax, baby,' Jayden said as he took possession of my nipple and sucked it to the rhythm of his thrusts. 'We are never going to hurt you.'

I looked back at Alex. Our eyes met and held. I felt him pushing his finger deeper into me. There was no pain and I found myself moving back into his finger. Jayden had stopped thrusting into me and was busy suckling on my nipples.

'Two?' Alex asked. I could see a tint of color on his face, from the strain of holding himself back.

I bit down on my lip and nodded, gasping as I felt another one of his fingers joining the one that was already inside. He gently moved his fingers in and out my asshole, increasing the tempo when he noticed me moving back on his fingers. When he added another finger I moaned out loud, pushed down on Jayden as well as Alex.

'Fuck!' Alex swore forcefully. 'I have to be inside you.'

I could only nod, holding my breath as he withdrew his hands and placed his manhood on the entrance of my asshole.

I was shaking so bad, moving my head I buried it on Jayden's shoulder.

'No, lioness,' Jayden slapped my butt. 'Look at him. Watch how he takes your ass.'

I shivered as I felt Alex pushing a bit into me. I did what Jayden commanded, turned my face and watched as Alex slowly pushed himself into me.

'Oh, lord,' I groaned as I felt him going deeper and deeper, his gaze never wavering from my face. I wanted so much to close my eyes and just feel but I also wanted to watch Alex, his cheeks tainted pink with effort.

'You can take all of me,' Alex said through gritted teeth as he pushed the last remaining inches into me.

For a few seconds they were both still, only Jayden's lips working on my nipples.

I felt a butterfly kiss on my shoulder, 'How do you feel?' Alex asked me as he gently withdrew and then pushed back.

I shook my head, 'full,' I replied, a small smile playing on my lips. 'Very full,' I moaned as this time both Alex and Jayden thrust into me. 'Oh lord!'

'That's it, baby,' Alex coaxed as he increased the tempo of his thrusts. 'Take it all.' He pushed into me, going deeper and deeper, as was Jayden. I could feel another orgasm building up. It started as a spark in my belly only to grow into an inferno.

I pushed back at them, s?ueezing my inner muscles and getting two groans as gifts. 'Oh my,' I whimpered as I felt the orgasm locking in and exploding.

'That's it, lioness,' Jayden breathed out as he too started to cum into my vagina. I could feel Alex's hands digging into my hips before he went still. Deep inside I felt a hot spray of his cum, and that triggered another orgasm.

I felt Alex collapsing behind me as my arms finally gave up supporting me and I slumped into Jayden. For the next minute or so, we did not speak; the room was full of ragged breathing from three people.

When finally, we were able to move, Alex removed himself from deep within and stood up. Walking to the bathroom, water running before he came back in.

CHAPTER 5

Jayden was in the process of moving me to the side, when Alex reached for me. It was amazing as to how these two guys were so in tune with each other. As I moved from Jayden's arms to Alex's, I smiled a little, hiding my face on the crook of his neck.

I watched as Jayden preceded us into the bathroom. It was already foggy with the hot water that was running.

'A shower first, then a soak in the tub,' Jayden said as he stepped into the shower first. Alex placed me down inside the cubicle before joining us in. As if he knew my legs were still not strong enough, he never released me from his grip.

Jayden moved closer, leaned forward and kissed me gently on my lips. As I moved into his arms, bring Alex closer too, something hard poked on my stomach. Looking down I smirked, 'round two?'

Jayden smiled, 'I thought you will never ask!'

I woke up feeling relaxed and trapped. The room was already flooded with the warm morning sunlight. A small smile escaped me as I felt Jayden stir from behind me. Pushing back into him, I heard his low groan before his arm tightened around my waist.

Feeling eyes on me, I looked up, coming to contact with blue eyes. A blush covered my cheeks from the hot gaze that Alex bestowed on me. He looked gorgeous, his hair tussled from sleep and my fingers from the previous night.

'Hi,' he mumbled, his finger tracing my jawline.

I smiled, 'hi,' I whispered back. I stretched a bit, feeling Jayden's arm tighten around me. Turning slightly, I blushed when he nuzzled my neck. I should really not be feeling horny and hot after the loving making from last night, but here I was, sandwiched between two men and I was ready for Round-I lost count.

Alex did not want to be left behind, moving lower and burying his face on my exposed breasts.

'Uhm, guys,' I whispered. 'Not that I do not want you this morning, but I am not comfortable with my morning breath.'

I felt Jayden laugh on my neck, the vibrations travelling to my toes. He placed a finger on my chin, turning me to his kiss. He was slow about it, thorough even. I groaned and gently pushed him away, 'morning breath!' I moved away from them, making my way to the bathroom. Opening the cabinets, I finally found spare toothbrushes. I frowned at that.

Why would they have a whole lot of toothbrushes? I asked myself as I brushed my teeth. After a rinse, I looked at myself in the mirror, trying to see if I have changed somehow.

'You still look good in the morning.'

I glanced at Jayden through the mirror. He was leaning on the doorframe, his arms crossed. I turned to him, leaning against the sink. I tilted my head, trying to gauge his emotions. I was naked, standing there in front of Jayden, who made no secret of his appraisal of my body. 'Thank you,' I mumbled, all of a sudden feeling shy.

As if reading my thoughts, he walked to where I was, placed his hands on either side of me before he leaned in and nuzzled my neck. I had to close my eyes as the sensations traveled through my body, waking up feelings that were taking a rest from the night before.

'Jay,' I mumbled. My hand traveled up from his arm to his chest, with full intention of pushing him away but instead I found I had no strength to do so. I rested my palm on his warm chest, feeling it seeping through into my body.

'Mmmh,' he moaned as his lips slowly traveled from my neck, slowly placing butterfly kisses on my jaw before he claimed my lips. His kiss was gentle yet demanding and I found myself responding to him even when I wanted to get into the shower first.

I closed my eyes, placing my arms around his neck as I pulled him closer for a deeper kiss. His hands roved on my body before coming to rest on my waist and pulling me deeper into his arms.

I gasped against his lips, feeling his heavy erection pushing against my tummy. Moaning low, I moved deeper into his arms, rubbing myself on him to entice him even more.

Jayden let go of my waist as his hands took a gentle hold of my head, holding me still for his ministrations. My own hands were now on his waist, holding him closer to me.

'Sky,' he groaned, as he broke the kiss and rested his forehead against mine. 'I want you so much I think I would burst if I don't have you right now!'

'Me too,' Alex's voice came through from the door. Past Jayden's shoulders, I watched as Alex walked slowly towards us, one of his hands gently stroking his erected member.

One Year Later...

'Look at that smile,' Taylor smiled as she sat next to me, pushing at me gently with her shoulder. We were at my house that Friday morning, one of the mornings where we were not so busy with our lives. The past year had been hectic in all our love lives. Taylor and Travis had decided to move in together. In all honesty I see wedding bells and the likes between the two of them. Taylor looked radiant and in love, and so did Travis when we met and we did meet a lot, with him being partners with Jayden and Alex.

Sasha and Landon were also another hot couple. Their romance was fiery from the word go. They have had their misunderstandings and fights, but emerged stronger than before.

'What?' I chuckled a little as I moved to make more space for her on the sofa.

She looked around my sitting room and sighed, 'well, you are halfway done with packing at least. How are you feeling?'

I stretched a little, rubbing my neck gently, 'tired! I just need a back massage, a foot massage and a twenty-four-hour nap.'

Taylor laughed as she stood up and walked to the table that had some drinks on it. 'What can I get you? Juice or water?'

'Wine, please,' I said with another sigh.

'Not going to happen,' she said as she poured two glasses of juice. Handing mine over to me, she took a sip from hers before settling it down. She was sitting on the floor before me. 'Your feet are swollen a bit,' she frowned. 'Have you gone to the doctor's? Is this normal? I knew it! You shouldn't have been doing this by yourself.'

'No, no, no,' I shook my head. 'Not you too, Tay! I already have to go through this with Jayden and Alex!' I wiggled my toes at her, 'it is normal for this amount of swelling. The doctor told me that my tissues are retaining some water and some other reason about the baby putting pressure on the uterus vein. It's no biggie,' I smiled at her. 'If it was, I would have gone to the hospital as fast as possible.'

Taylor sighed, her hand going to her own stomach. I frowned as I watched her rubbing her tummy gently, the same way I used to rub mine when I was newly pregnant. When she caught my eye, she quickly removed her hand and averted her eyes.

'Taylor Benjamin, is there something you want to tell me?' I asked as I moved up slowly.

'What makes you think I want to tell you anything?'

I raised an eyebrow, 'how about the fact that you were rubbing your tummy so momsy like right now. And not to mention you passed a chance of drinking one of the best wines from Alex's collection and opted for Orange juice, which you do not really fancy.' When she kept quiet I nudged her with my toes. 'I am waiting!'

'Alright!' she rolled her eyes. 'I am about two months along. We just got it confirmed a week ago.'

I squealed with happiness, struggling with my tummy to hug her from where she was seated before me. 'I am so happy for you! Travis must be over the moon!'

Taylor chuckled, 'he is ecstatic. We wanted to wait until we're married and all, but I guess we are sort of married, having been living together for the past eight months!'

'I still want to be a bridesmaid, so that nonsense of being already married is not going to stick,' I rubbed on my tummy, 'well, make sure it's after this little one comes out.'

Taylor smiled and stood up from where she was sitting on the floor. Taking a seat beside me, she placed her hand on my bulging tummy. 'Not long to go now, about 2 months, yeah?'

I nodded, 'but sleeping has become an issue! The other night I chased the guys out of the bed with my tossing and turning.'

Taylor shook her head, 'I still find it weird to think that you are in love with two men, and that they have no issue sharing you.'

I sighed and closed my eyes, a smile playing on my lips, 'I know. If I were you, I would not believe it as well. It was difficult at first, with me trying to put them both in the same box. But as time went by, I learnt to see them as two different men, two men that I loved unconditionally and they loved me in their own different ways.'

Alex, who was the dominant one when it came to my relationship with him, had made sure I stopped working three months after I found out I was pregnant, but not before I was done with the renovations on his mother's cottage.

Jayden was the more relaxed one of them; he was the one who instead of ordering me, wanted my opinion. When I wanted to be spoilt rotten, Jayden was the man to go to, when I wanted to feel safe and secured, Alex was the one I turned to.

'Enough about the serious talk,' I struggled to my feet, collecting my handbag by the coffee table. 'Let's get out of the house for a while. Packing can be so depressing.'

'Still can't believe that it has taken you this long to pack up this house!' Taylor shook her head.

I shrugged, 'I am a sentimentalist, what can I say?'

'Where are we going?' Taylor shook her head as she followed me out of the house.

I shrugged, 'craving some fish at the moment, so we are going where the fish is. You are driving. Alex does not want me behind the wheel; he dropped me over today and will come to pick me up in the evening.' As we made our way to the car, my phone started to vibrate in my handbag. 'Speaking of the devil,' I muttered as I showed Taylor the flashing name on my screen. 'Hello, darling.'

'Hi,' he replied with a voice sexy enough to send shivers down my spine. 'How are you doing? Are you taking it slow?'

'We are excellent. Actually Tay stopped by and now we are heading out to get some fish. I am craving some buttered calamari.'

Alex laughed, 'alright, will check you later. Have fun with Taylor. I love you.'

'Will do,' I smiled. 'Love you too.'

Taylor shook her head as she put the car into gear, 'those men of yours know how to spoil you.'

I shrugged with a goofy smile on my face.

The restaurant that Taylor chose was right close to the ocean, and the food there was great. After ordering a fish platter, we sat back enjoying our own company.

'Well, well, look who we have here,' a woman whom I have never seen before remarked as she stood beside our table, crossing her arms before her and shooting daggers at me with her eyes.

'Sorry,' Taylor sat back, looking over at the woman. 'But do we know you?'

'I am not interested in you,' she turned her deep grey eyes to Taylor, discarding her as though she was a piece of used napkin. 'You on the other hand, you tickle my curiosity.'

'I do?' I frowned. 'How?'

She smiled, her smile reminding me of a shark ready to bite, 'for starters is how you can be in a relationship with two men at the same time?'

I could feel my face being drained out of blood. Taking a deep breath, I shook my head, 'I don't follow.'

'Don't act stupid, it's useless to me,' she waved her hand as if chasing away my answer. 'I know you stay in the same house with two men, men who have had rumors of their unconventional lifestyles. Do you deny this?'

I tilted my head a bit, taking in the woman before me. It all clicked at that time. Smiling a little, I shook my head. 'Deny that I live in the same house with two men? Why would I do that? It is the truth.'

'And the fact you are in a relationship with both of them?'

'It's already a fact? I never knew that,' I shrugged. 'It seems you are interested in my relationships, right? It has me interested in yours as well. How many men are you in a relationship with at the moment?'

'That is none of your business!' she scratched.

'Exactly,' I nodded. 'Who I am having a relationship with or lack of it is none of your concern. You can go to someone else to get a scoop for your tabloid, television show or your YouTube channel but not me. And the next time you come to me and harass me while I am out minding my own business be ready for a lawsuit that will have you begging by the corner of this restaurant. As you said, I do live with two men, and judging by the way you spoke about them, I am sure you know how well they like to protect their privacy.'

'Are you threatening me? You chose your life; they are well known people so of course people would like to know about their lives.'

'No, I am not threatening you. I am telling you,' I corrected her. 'Yes, people would like to know about their lives, but if they do not want it to be known it's their prerogative, just as it is mine. I suggest you run along and find some other front page news hungry fanatic and leave me alone.'

'You have not seen the last of me,' she warned.

I took in a deep breath and stood up, my tummy leading. 'Now I am going to threaten you. Be very careful who you harass, girly, because some of us can make your life very tough. I can have you fired from your job; make sure that no other newspaper-no matter how small-hires you, all your contacts will evaporate. You will find earth to be very small, tiny even. You threaten me, my privacy, you threaten my health. Imagine if I tell the father of this child that you have been harassing me, following me around, asking me stressful ⍰uestions? Tell me, what do you think he'll do? Mind you, you do not know who it is, but I am sure that their reputations precede them. You know how ruthless they get.'

The woman narrowed her eyes, triumph shining in her grey eyes. 'You do not even know who I am. Your threats are empty.'

'I do,' Taylor spoke up, giving her a smile. 'You are Camille Robertson, working for that weekly tabloid that has had more lawsuits than sales. I believe the state as given them one more chance, if you have one more scandal, your paper will be shut down, as you will not be able to afford it. Already the paper is running on red.'

For the first time, Camille's face lost its color, 'you wouldn't.'

'Try me,' I replied calmly. 'As I said, find someone else who is front page news hungry and stalk them. As for me, the moment I see you, I will not hesitate to report you to the father of my baby, and I am sure you really don't want that.'

Camille shook her head, 'you know, I thought you were going to be an easy story to get, but I guess I was wrong.'

I returned to my seat, 'you bet I am not easy. And I would appreciate if you pass the word around to anyone else who might think of me that way. You want to write about my interior designing, great I will give you all the tips you need. If you want to write about Alex and Jayden, I am sure you know where they work, go to them. But don't you dare write about what you think will sell more, you will be sorry.'

Camille gave me a small smile, 'ok, I get you. One last question before I go.'

I shot her a dark gaze.

'It's a work habit!' she raised her hands in defeat. 'Who is the father of your child?'

I tilted my head to the side, a small smile playing on my lips, 'it's a man.'

'But-?'

'That's all you are getting,' I turned back to Taylor who was looking at me with laughter in her eyes.

For a few seconds Camille just stood there, as though expecting me to give her more than what I had said. When she figured I was not going to talk she sighed and walked away, giving me the space to finally sigh.

'Girly!' Taylor burst out laughing. 'She is older than you!'

'Oh, God!' I murmured as I hid my face behind my hands.

Taylor continued laughing, 'you are a small dynamite stick, aren't you, doll?'

I peeped at her through my fingers as I shook my head, 'I don't know what came over me!'

'Hey,' Taylor reached out and took my hands from my face, holding them in hers, 'you defended your privacy, that's what you did. And I am so proud of you!'

'I threatened her!' I lowered my voice. 'That wasn't nice.'

'And her trying to make a living for selling other people's private lives isn't nice. Look, Sky, you have to be tough sometimes and these are some of those times. Don't feel bad about it, ok. I would have punched her in the face. Or if you want to know that you handled that much better, think about what Sasha could have done!'

I laughed as I closed my eyes, 'we would have been bailing her from jail right about now.'

'Exactly,' Taylor smiled, tilting her head to the side. 'One thing I am curious about though that she mentioned is who the father of the baby is. Do you know?'

I laughed, 'of course I do. And no, I will not tell you how.'

Two years Later

'Guys, will you please hurry up!' I called from the bottom of the stairs. 'We are running extremely late!' I walked to the front door, stood beside it and waited for Jayden and Alex to come down. A smile broke on my face when both of my men came down carrying a child in their arms.

'Dressing these two is like World War Zero!' Jayden stated as he lifted the little giggling girl in his arms.

'At least she does not run around like Caleb,' Alex murmured as he tickled the boy he was holding in his arms. 'Thank goodness, it'll be your turn to dress him up later on after we come back from Sasha's wedding.'

I shook my head, 'are you two still complaining? I do this all the time!'

Yes, you read right. I am now the mother of two toddlers, a beautiful three-month old baby girl named Zuriel after my mother and a handsome twenty-month old boy named Caleb. They were the apples of my eyes, and from the looks of it, they were also the apple of their fathers' eyes

Alex and Jayden treated the children equally, even though it was obvious that Caleb was Jayden's and Zuriel was Alex's daughter. We had planned it all along. Because I was with Jayden first and he had always wanted to be a father, it was only fair that he be the first one to be called dad. Alex had wanted to learn first, but the moment Caleb came into the world, he had changed his mind, wanting a child as fast as possible.

It was pretty simple actually. The men kept a close follow-up on my calendar, making sure that only Jayden touched me during my fertile period and only he and I could make love without any protection until I fell pregnant, the same went for Alex.

Alex stopped in front of me, leaning forward to claim my lips with his. It was a demanding kiss, just the way Alex had always done things. He lifted his free hand to my neck, bunching my hair on my nape so he could deepen the kiss. 'And we are always left awed by it,' he mumbled against
my lips before letting me go.

I smiled at him, my fingers running against the seam of his lips before I turned my gaze to Caleb, 'naughty boy, you are supposed to be walking by yourself and not letting daddy carry you,' I tickled his tummy, rubbing my nose on his.

Caleb chuckled and reached for me, opening his arms out so that I could take him.

Alex shook his head as he walked away with Caleb, 'oh no, buddy. It's to the car with you.'

Jayden laughed as Caleb started his complaining. 'I wonder where he gets his argumentative character from. Do you happen to know?' he said as he ran a finger on my jaw line.

An eyebrow went up, as I looked at him, 'I don't know what you are talking about.' I smiled as he mirrored my eyebrow lift before he too, reached for me. His kiss was gentle, coaxing a response from me with nips on my lips. A giggle escaped me when Zuriel decided that I had had enough attention from her father number two. With a gentle peck on my lips, Jayden tightened his hold on Zuriel before walking to the waiting car.

Making sure that the doors were locked I followed suit, taking my front seat next to Jayden who had left the strapping in of our daughter to Alex, I buckled up before twisting and turning to the back to look at Alex and our two children.

'Everyone ready?' Jayden asked as he put the car into gear.

'Yep!' Caleb chuckled from his seat, clapping his hands as always when he was in the car. I laughed at his big smile, so infectious that had both men smiling along. 'Go, go, go!' those were his favourite words.

'You heard the man,' Alex drawled. 'Let's go and see Sasha finally getting married. Landon had to work really hard to convince her.'

Jayden laughed, 'Sasha is a firecracker.'

I laughed, 'I think with both Taylor and I settled, Sasha felt left out, especially when we start talking about babies.'

Taylor had given birth to a beautiful baby girl, exactly six months after me. She had been shocked when I had announced that I was pregnant again, so was Sasha. But that was the way we had planned it. We did not want too many years or months between Jayden's and Alex's babies. We had agreed two for Jayden and two for Alex, but these will come after a few years.

'Well, at least now she will finally have a ring on her finger,' Jayden smiled as he turned the car, directing it to the main road.

A smile broke off on my lips as I caught Alex's gaze. For a few seconds we stared at each other before his eyes moved to my left hand that was resting on my thigh. Reaching forward, he grabbed it and pulled it towards his lips, all the while holding my gaze. Placing a kiss on the two rings I had on, he turned my hand before placing another kiss on my palm.

Now, you might think the two rings were my wedding and engagement rings, if you think so then you are wrong. They are both my wedding rings.

How, you ask? It's simple. Both Jayden and Alex gave me wedding rings, though not on the same day. I guess this is the hardest sacrifice in our relationship, not being able to marry both men that I love. I could only marry one, and that was Jayden Not saying that Alex was free to be with whoever he wanted, no. I was married to him too, only that marriage did not have the blessings of a church, magistrate, imam or whoever gave blessings at weddings.

The marriage between Alex and I was all about the commitment we had for each other. Yes, Jayden was my legal husband; his name was on our marriage certificate. We went through the whole process of weddings, invited close friends and family, said our "I dos" and promised to share all our forever together but Alex was never far from us.

In fact, Alex was the best man. During the exchanging of my vows with Jayden, Alex had moved closer, just as we had planned, so I could include him somehow. Saying the vows that I had written for that special occasion, I had made sure that when I said them, Alex would know that I was saying them to him too.

I had only found out later on during the celebrations that Alex and Jayden had sat down together to come up with vows to say to me.

Anyway, we were talking about my two wedding rings. During our honeymoon, on one of the private islands in Greece, Alex had decided that he wanted me to wear his ring as well. He had gone out with Jayden, leaving me satisfied after a bounty of love-making on the pretense of giving me time to rest before they were back and it was back to the lovemaking.

When they had finally arrived, instead of the love-making I was promised, I was ordered by him to dress up in what he had bought for me and meet them at one of the many gazebos populating the island. Coaxing information from Jayden was useless, as he kept on telling me I would love the surprise.

Walking down the stairs to the gazebo, I had no idea what was happening. I had found my two men, dressed in matching tuxedos waiting for me. Alex had moved forward, taking my hand in his and led me further into the gazebo. The sun was setting, so the ambiance was beautiful.

'What's going on?' I had asked, a curious smile playing on my lips. 'Jayden?' I turned to him, as he stood a bit further than Alex and I.

Jayden smiled and shook his head, 'I love you, lioness, but this is Alex's time. Ask him.'

I had turned to Alex then, watching him as he led me to the Centre of the gazebo. Getting there he had turned me in his arms, pulling me to him and bestowing a lingering kiss on my lips.

'I love you,' he had whispered against my lips.

I smiled, 'I love you too, Alex. You know that.' I moved away a bit, getting my hands free from his so I could frame his face. 'I always will.'

He had pulled me back into his arms, deepening the kiss until we were both breathless. Breaking it, he had rested his forehead on mine, eyes closed.

I had frowned a bit, 'Alex, you are scaring me. What's wrong? You are not leaving me, are you?' The thought of losing him had pierced my heart causing tears to flood my eyes. 'You can't leave me! You, Jayden and Caleb are my family and I need all of you.'

'No!' he had denied furiously, 'what made you think I would ever leave you?'

I had shrugged, trying to blink away the tears.

'I will never leave you, darling, ever! I brought you here because I wanted to give you something. I know we had agreed that Jayden be your legal husband, but I also want to be your husband as well.'

'You already are,' I had reached up to his cheek again. 'The vows I had said were for the both of you.'

Alex had taken hold of my hand, placing a kiss on my palm, 'I know. But I want to say mine to you. Right here, right now. And on top of Jayden's ring, I want you to wear mine as well.'

I had smiled then, pulling him to me. 'Of course.'

And that is how I got to have two wedding rings. Do people think it's crazy, I don't know, and I really do not care. My friends that matter, Taylor and Sasha have been with me from the beginning and they know that I am in a relationship with both men. They also know that Caleb is Jayden's and Zuriel is Alex's, but they have never judged me. What is the difference between me and those women and men who have more than one partner? Whereas they choose to keep their extra partners a secret, I choose to make mine public. Yes, I sleep with both men, sometimes on the same bed, sometimes individually. Yes, we do have arguments, all couples do, but my fight with Alex has nothing to do with Jayden, nor does my fight with Jayden have anything to do with Alex.

For those who know about our relationship and judge us, we do not make time for them. At the end of the day it's all about us and how happy we are. We love each other, we are a family.

*******END*******

Hope you enjoy reading this book. Kindly leave a feedback on amazon, this will mean a lot to me.

Thanks.

39661838R00117

Printed in Poland
by Amazon Fulfillment
Poland Sp. z o.o., Wrocław